# OPERATION: SAVE THE TEACHER

## WEDNESDAY NIGHT MATCH

*Other Avon Camelot Books in the*
**OPERATION: SAVE THE TEACHER** *Series*
*by Meg Wolitzer*

TUESDAY NIGHT PIE

*Coming Soon*

SATURDAY NIGHT TOAST

MEG WOLITZER grew up on Long Island and now lives in New York City with her husband and son. She is the author of several books for adults and young readers, including *Caribou* and *The Dream Book*.

# OPERATION: SAVE THE TEACHER

## WEDNESDAY NIGHT MATCH

MEG WOLITZER

OPERATION: SAVE THE TEACHER: WEDNESDAY NIGHT MATCH is an original publication of Avon Books. This work has never before appeared in book form.

AVON BOOKS
A division of
The Hearst Corporation
1350 Avenue of the Americas
New York, New York 10019


Published by arrangement with the author
Library of Congress Catalog Card Number: 92-97301
ISBN: 0-380-76461-X
RL: 5.0



First Avon Camelot Printing: May 1993

CAMELOT TRADEMARK REG. U.S. PAT. OFF. AND IN OTHER COUNTRIES, MARCA REGISTRADA, HECHO EN U.S.A.

Printed in the U.S.A.

OPM 10 9 8 7 6 5 4 3 2 1

To Helen and Chester Panek

# Chapter One

When Julie Hopwood got dressed on the morning of the first day of sixth grade, she found a surprise waiting for her in her sock drawer. Every year on the first day of school her mother hid a present somewhere in Julie's room. Last year it had been a tiny unicorn carved of wood and hidden inside her pencil box; the year before it had been hidden in one of Julie's shoes. She had slipped her foot in, only to find a lump at the toe. The lump had been a silver ring with the letter *J* on it.

But this morning, when Julie went to pick out a pair of socks, she found a flat white box tied up with red ribbon. On the box was a card, which read, "To My Sixth-Grader." Julie pulled at the ribbon and then fumbled quickly with the box. Even though she was very sleepy, she still felt excited whenever she found one of her mother's surprises.

Inside the box was a little purple notebook. Why would her mother give her a notebook? she wondered. They had already gone shopping for school supplies the week before; Julie's new multisubject notebook was still blank and waiting inside her knapsack. Now Julie stood and flipped through the notebook. It was pretty, she realized, with a delicate pattern of purple flowers on the cover; it wasn't the kind of notebook you could rip the pages out of.

"You found it!"

Julie looked up. Her mother was standing in the doorway, dressed in a bathrobe and holding a coffee cup.

"Yeah, I did," said Julie. "Thanks, Mom. It's really nice. But what's it for?"

"Oh," said her mother, "I just thought you might want to start a journal this year. You're in sixth grade now, and I thought maybe you were old enough."

"You mean like a diary?" Julie asked.

"In a way," said her mother. "Just a place to write down your thoughts. Anything that occurs to you. Anything you might want to remember later on."

Ms. Hopwood was a writer. She wrote novels and taught writing at the local university two afternoons a week. Her books always contained real things that had happened to the Hopwood family, only in the books, the family wasn't called the Hopwoods—they were called the Hathaways. Her first novel was about how the Hathaway parents had met each other and fallen in love, then had two children and moved from New York City to Iowa City. In the second book, Mr. and Ms. Hathaway got divorced, and Mr. Hathaway moved to California. Julie had only skimmed that book; she didn't really want to read about such things. When her own parents had gotten divorced, her father had moved to Los Angeles, and she saw him only twice a year when he came to visit.

The last time he had come had been during Julie's spring vacation. When they walked down the snowy Iowa streets together, she noticed that he looked different from everybody else, with his skin tanned a rosy brown. Sometimes, when she tried to picture him, all she could see was the tan.

Julie sat down at the table, and her mother put out an array of dry cereal boxes in front of her. Ms. Hopwood almost never cooked. She didn't have that much time to cook, and even when she did, her meals never came out great. She was nothing like Julie's friend Trina's mother, who was a wonderful cook, and whose chicken pot pies were selling well in supermarkets all over the state.

"So what will it be?" Ms. Hopwood asked. "Rice Chex? Total?"

"How about Crunchy Whizzers?" asked Dennis, padding into the kitchen in his slippers that looked like furry bear claws.

"No, we are *not* going to have Crunchy Whizzers," said Ms. Hopwood. "That stuff is 100 percent sugar."

"Not true, Mom, not true," said Dennis. He took a seat at the table. "In addition to sugar, Crunchy Whizzers are also made up of calcium carbonate, trisodium phosphate, corn syrup, and artificial coloring."

"My little Einstein," said Ms. Hopwood. "Do you know the answer to everything?

"No, but I try," said Dennis. He flashed a big, bratty smile. Dennis Hopwood was considered by everyone to be the smartest kid in Lily Abernathy Elementary School. He was nine years old and about to start fourth grade.

"I hope you'll both take notes in your new journals," said Ms. Hopwood over breakfast.

So she had bought Dennis a notebook too! Julie felt a little disappointed; usually, their first-day-of-school gifts were completely different, but this year their mother had bought them the same thing. Instead of purple flowers on the cover, Dennis's had pictures of tiny green spaceships. What would Dennis possibly write in his journal?

Julie wondered. *"E = mc*$^2$*"?* She couldn't even begin to imagine.

"Mom got me a journal too," Julie told her brother.

"Oh," said Dennis. "What are you going to write, anyway? Love letters to Mr. Graham?" He started to laugh.

Mr. Graham had been Julie's fifth-grade teacher the year before. He was the nicest teacher in school, and very handsome too, with reddish hair the color of an Irish setter. His wife had been killed in a car accident when Julie was in his class, and she and her group of friends had rallied around and tried to help him. They had babysat for his two kids after school, and cleaned his house and done a little cooking. It hadn't worked out too well, though: first there had been a big kitchen explosion, which left rice pudding and shattered glass all over the walls and the ceiling, and later, Mr. Graham's daughter Anna had hidden inside the washing machine and no one could find her, which had made Mr. Graham turn pale and almost faint. Anna had turned up safe and sound, but still, it was all a bit much for Mr. Graham. He had fired the girls, but then in the end he had softened and given them a second chance during the summer.

Julie and her friends had spent July and August helping out around their teacher's house.

Actually, he wasn't their teacher anymore, but what did you call someone who had once been your teacher but no longer was? Julie had heard her mother refer to Julie's father as her "ex-husband." Maybe that was what Mr. Graham was: their ex-teacher.

Julie had a secret about Mr. Graham, which really wasn't much of a secret at all, because all her friends knew, and so, apparently, did her brother Dennis, who teased her about it whenever he had a chance. The secret was that Julie had a crush on Mr. Graham. He was the kind of person she hoped she would meet one day when she was older, and maybe fall in love with. He was gentle and funny and really listened when you talked, unlike the boys at school who told fart jokes and made you feel like something was wrong with you all the time. It was hard to imagine that those boys would ever grow up to become half as nice as Mr. Graham, or even half as good-looking.

Julie almost never talked about her crush on Mr. Graham; it was just one of those facts that hovered around the edges of her daily life, and occasionally she would remember that it was there. She didn't lie awake at night thinking about him, and she'd certainly never written him a love letter, but sometimes over the summer, when she had been helping out around his house, she would think: *This is Mr. Graham's house I'm in,* and the thought would make her very happy, as though her life and his overlapped a little.

"No, I'm *not* going to write love letters to Mr. Graham," she said to Dennis in a big-sister voice. "I'm going to keep a journal, and write about things that are important to me."

"Yeah, well, that's exactly what *I'm* going to do," said Dennis.

"Copycat," said Julie.

"I think it's great that you're both going to keep journals," said Ms. Hopwood, sensing that a fight was brewing between her kids. "I'm sure a lot of interesting things will happen to each of you this year. It's a good idea to write it all down, so you can remember it later on."

But Julie wondered what sort of interesting things could possibly happen to her this year. After all, she wasn't going to be in Mr. Graham's class anymore; she was going to be in Mrs. Leff's class. When you were in Mr. Graham's class, you could be sure something interesting would happen. But Mrs. Leff was new. Nobody had met her yet, so no one knew if she was young or old, short or tall, nice or mean. But her name was strange: *Leff.* What kind of a name was that anyway? Julie preferred the name *Graham,* which made her think of graham crackers, one of her favorite foods.

It didn't seem likely that anything too interesting was going to happen this year. Iowa City was a pretty good place to live, although a lot of farms in the area had been sold in recent years, and people were out of work. On the school bus every morning, Julie rode past acres of flat land. Iowa City was far away from places where things really happened—places like Los Angeles.

Julie had never been to Los Angeles, but in all the photographs her father sent, it looked very exciting and pretty. There were big, exotic trees that reminded Julie of pineapples, and wide streets with expensive stores, and glistening foreign cars with license plates that read I Luv Ya and Smooch.

Here in Iowa City, Julie's mother drove a green station wagon that had all sorts of odds and ends rolling around in the back and under the seats. It was like a big pocketbook—loose change at the bottom, and gum wrappers, and a few ancient raisins that were now covered with dog hair. The Hopwoods' house looked like the inside of an even bigger pocketbook, filled with papers and books and shoes. Ms. Hopwood wasn't very big on straightening up, which made life pretty easy, because she never yelled at Julie or Dennis to clean up their rooms. But there were times when Julie wished the house was just a little neater. She usually felt this way when her group of friends came over after school. She always felt as though she had to apologize for the way the house looked. The place wasn't dirty—that is, covered with grime or grease—but things were just never where you expected them to be. You might find a pair of socks wedged between the stove and refrigerator, or Ms. Hopwood's keys on the floor beneath the TV. But for some reason, Julie's friends loved spending time at the Hopwoods' house.

Ms. Hopwood collected antiques; back when she and Julie's father were still married, they would all go to flea markets on weekends. Flea markets were big fairs where people set up folding tables and spread out things to sell: jewelry, vases, old comic books, baseball cards, furniture, and everything else you could imagine. On the way home from the flea market, the back of the station wagon would always be full. On the ride home, Julie's father would make up dumb songs about the things they had bought that day:

*"Oh I went to the flea market*
*To buy my flea a flute*
*But all the good stuff was taken*
*And not one flute would toot*
*So I went to another flea market*
*To buy my flea a lamp*
*But it rained so hard the whole day long*
*That every flea lamp was damp. . . ."*

Thinking of the flea market song now, as she

sat at the breakfast table with Dennis and her mother, Julie felt sad. She had trouble even remembering what her father's voice sounded like, although he called every week. But telephones made everything sound funny and distant; often she felt as though she was talking to her father through a seashell.

Sometimes she couldn't get over how much everything had changed in her life already, and she was barely in sixth grade. Once her parents had been married and the whole family had gone to flea markets. Once her father had lived with them in Iowa. Once Julie had been a fifth-grader. Once Mr. Graham had been her teacher. All those things had changed; not one of them was the same anymore.

"What's the matter, Julie?" her mother asked her now. "It's the first day of school. You *love* school. Why do you look so down?"

Julie shrugged. "I don't know," she said.

"Is it about Mr. Graham?" Ms. Hopwood asked. "Is it because he's not going to be your teacher this year?"

"Yeah, I guess that's part of it," said Julie.

"Well, you'll still see him every day," said her mother. "And didn't he tell you and your friends that you were all welcome to visit him and his kids at their house sometime?"

"Yes," said Julie.

"Are you worried that you won't like your new teacher as much?" asked Ms. Hopwood.

"Yeah," said Julie.

"I've got a great teacher!" piped up Dennis. "Her name is Mrs. Liebert and she plays the guitar! Every year she picks a day to be Chocolate Day, and she lets her whole class bring in chocolate and eat as much of it as they want!"

"Yeah, well good for you," said Julie. "I hope you and your whole class break out in pimples from all that chocolate."

"*I'm* not the one with pimples," Dennis said happily.

"Oh, kids," said Ms. Hopwood. "Does every day have to start off like this? Can there ever be a little peace around here?"

Just then the doorbell rang. Julie leapt to her feet. She could see through the frosted glass that it was her best friend, Alison Spaeth, waiting on the front step to walk with her to the bus stop. Alison was tall and had dark hair and an easy, open smile. She was the best friend Julie had ever had in her life. She and Alison told each other everything, but they also just liked being together and *not* talking—working on homework or watching TV.

"Saved by the bell," said Ms. Hopwood.

"I've got to run," said Julie, and she stood up.

"Can't you at least wait for your brother?" her mother asked.

"I can walk by myself," said Dennis. "I've got a patella and a femur and a tibia."

"You've got *what?*" Julie asked.

"For your information, those happen to be the names of the bones in your legs," said Dennis, and he triumphantly finished his cereal.

"Mr. Know-it-all," Julie muttered.

She kissed her mother good-bye and was almost at the door, when she suddenly remembered something. She went back into the kitchen. "I almost forgot," she said.

"What?" asked her mother.

"This," said Julie, and she picked up the journal her mother had given her. Then she quickly slipped it into her knapsack and headed for the door.

# Chapter Two

*Dear Journal,*

*Are you supposed to say "Dear Journal," the way you say "Dear Diary"? I think "Dear Journal" looks a little weird. My mother says that a journal is different from a diary. She says a diary is a place where you write down really secret things, but a journal is a place where you keep track of all the thoughts you have about anything you feel like writing about.*

*So today, which was the first day of school, I am going to write down all the things that happened to me as well as all the things I thought about. I am not a very good writer, so please excuse the dumbness that may creep in every now and then. My mother is the writer in the family. My father is the lawyer. And my brother is the genius. As for me, I'm not sure what I am: there isn't one thing that people think of when they think of me. Right now the only thing that occurs to me is that I am a sixth-grader. Which is something I've never been before. . . .*

When school started, Julie was glad to see all the same faces from last year. Some kids had different haircuts, and almost everyone had new clothes on; the colors were still really bright from not being washed yet, and you could see the creases in the boys' pants from where they had been lying on a shelf in a department store. Julie stood with her best friend, Alison, in the playground with Trina Alberts, Susan Moseby, and Stacy Geller. Trina had brought along a bag of apple raisin minimuffins that her mother had baked that morning, and the girls all stood around eating them before the bell rang.

The boys were standing by the fire doors and joking in loud voices. Adam Lewin was taller, and Danny Behnke, who was tough and a little scary, looked almost as big as a high school kid. There was a little bit of dark fuzz above his lip that almost looked like a mustache, if you squinted.

All of the students who had been in Mr. Graham's class the year before were now splitting up and going into different classes. Alison was going to be in Mrs. Nero's class. She and Julie wouldn't be able to sit together; they wouldn't be able to work on projects together, or whisper, or do their homework together after school. In fact, not many of Julie's friends were in Mrs. Leff's class with her. Trina was in Mr. Hilburn's class. The only one of her good friends who would be in class with her was Susan.

When the bell rang, everyone piled in through the doors. The halls seemed a little narrower than last year, and the overhead lights seemed brighter than Julie remembered. There were no paintings up on the walls yet, and no posters. The whole place was very clean.

"Doesn't it look weird?" Julie asked Alison.

"Yeah," Alison said. "It's like a school in a dream."

Julie knew exactly what her best friend meant. As if she were in a dream, she walked by Mr. Graham's classroom. Through the windows she could see him inside, sitting on his desk. There were a few kids standing around him, and he was chatting with them. Julie wanted to be in that room so much! She wanted to have Mr. Graham as a teacher, and she wanted to sit in that class and listen to him talk five days a week, from now until June. He was wearing a white shirt and a green checked tie, and his hair was as red as ever, and Julie thought he looked great. Last year, after his wife had been killed in a car accident, he had looked very tired and worn out for a while, as if he didn't get any sleep at night. But over the summer, when Julie and the other girls helped Mr. Graham out around the house and took care of his kids, they could tell that he was getting back to his old self. And now today, the first day of school, he looked perfect.

The only problem was, Julie wasn't going to be there to see him. She had to continue walking down the hall and then turn right to get to her new classroom. Alison had to make a left to go to Mrs. Nero's room.

"Well, bye," Alison said.

"Bye," said Julie.

They just stood there looking at each other. All around them kids were streaming down the hall, heading for their classrooms. "It's not like we're going off to *war* or anything," said Alison. "We're just going to be in different rooms, that's all."

"I know," said Julie. "But it feels like we'll never see each other, doesn't it?"

"Yeah," Alison admitted.

Then Julie had an idea. "I know," she said. "Every day at eleven o'clock, we'll both ask our teachers if we can be excused to go to the water fountain. And that way we can be sure we'll see each other. We'll be able to talk for a minute at the water fountain."

"Great!" said Alison. "You think of the best

things. You're so creative. Just like your mother. The only thing is, don't you think we should change the exact time we get water every day? Otherwise, our teachers might get suspicious."

"You're right," said Julie, and they arranged that this morning, they would meet at the water fountain at exactly 11:08. "Well," she said. "Good luck in Mrs. Nero's class." But Alison wouldn't really need any luck; Mrs. Nero had been teaching at the school for a long time, and everybody said she was very nice.

Julie headed for her new classroom. She saw a few other kids go inside; some of them she knew very well, others barely at all. She was sorry to see that Danny Behnke was in her class. He took a seat in the last row, and leaned all the way back in his chair, tipping it up in that way that teachers hated. Teachers were always saying that if you sat like that, you would fall backward and break your neck, but Julie didn't know a single person who had ever broken his neck doing that. She was sure it had happened in some school, somewhere, but not here.

Susan sat beside Julie now and immediately lined up her pens and pencils on her desktop. She was the neatest person Julie had ever met. "Have you seen Mrs. Leff yet?" Susan asked when she had put out the last pen and pencil.

"No," said Julie. "No one has."

The front of the room was empty. The chair at the teacher's desk was still pushed in, and the only things on the surface of the desk were a heavy gray stapler, a Scotch tape dispenser, and a little glass jar full of paper clips. "Maybe she won't show up," said Susan.

"She has to," said Julie. "It's the first day of school."

Just then the second bell rang, and at that very moment, the door of the classroom was pushed open, and in walked Mrs. Leff. She looked like a teacher on a TV show—really young and pretty with a light blue sweater draped around her shoulders. She wore eyeglasses with red designer frames that looked good on her. She looked like the kind of teacher you could feel relaxed with. Maybe she would celebrate Chocolate Day, like Dennis's teacher, or at least her version of it: Ice Cream Day, or Jelly Bean Day. Julie and Susan looked at each other and nodded their heads slightly, as if to say: So far, so good.

But things turned out to be very different. Mrs. Leff sat down behind her desk and folded her hands on the clean blotter, and said, "Well! Good morning, class. My name is Mrs. Leff and I will be your teacher this year. I have been teaching over at the Harry Truman Grade School in Kansas City, Kansas, for the past four years, and let me tell you, the boys and girls in that school were extremely polite and responsible. Each and every one of them paid attention to the lessons I taught, and did their homework assignments every night. They were model students, and I only hope that you boys and girls will be model students too."

Susan and Julie looked at each other. Model students? That meant perfect. Julie felt very nervous all of a sudden, and she noticed that all around her, the other kids looked nervous too. It was as if everyone was thinking about how Mrs. Leff wanted them to be perfect, and nobody knew if the class was up it.

The rest of the morning was spent passing out textbooks and figuring out who would sit where. Class monitors were chosen, and dittos were handed out about Colonial America. Julie loved the smell of new ditto sheets, and as soon as hers was passed to her, she lifted it up in front of her face and inhaled. When she put the sheet of paper down, Mrs. Leff was already onto a new topic: neatness. "In Kansas City," she said, "my students won the award for cleanest classroom. The principal came to our room and pasted up a gold seal on the wall!" She smiled, as though her new class would think this was the most wonderful thing in the world, as though they were staring at that blazing gold seal at that very minute.

Suddenly Julie realized that it was already

11:07—time to meet Alison at the water fountain. She raised her hand and asked to be excused. Mrs. Leff looked at her as though she had asked a really big favor, and then she paused, as though deciding what to do.

"Well, all right," Mrs. Leff finally said. "But hurry back, Julia. We have a lot to do."

Julia. No one ever called her that. Julie left the classroom, relieved to be out of there. As she turned the corner, she saw Alison in the distance, hovering around the water fountain.

"You're late," Alison said when she got there. "Every time someone walked past, I had to take another drink of water. I must have drunk a gallon already!"

"Well, then you'll probably spend the rest of the morning asking to be excused to go to the bathroom," said Julie, and they both laughed. Another teacher walked by, and this time Julie was the one to lean over the water fountain. A short squirt of warm water spurted up. It was like drinking a bath. Suddenly Julie thought to herself that the water fountains in that elementary school in Kansas City were really perfect, with freezing-cold water leaping up in a tall, bold spray whenever anyone pressed the button.

"So how's Mrs. Leff?" Alison asked when Julie was done.

Julie wiped her mouth. "Well," she said, "she's

nothing like Mr. Graham. She's really nervous, and she just goes on and on about her last class in Kansas City, and how wonderful they were. I mean, she tries to be nice and everything, but it's like she's teaching at a military school. You know how Mr. Graham is? She's kind of the opposite of that."

"Well, that's too bad," said Alison.

"How's Mrs. Nero?" Julie asked.

"Exactly what you'd expect," said Alison. "Really nice. Kind of slow-moving, though. Like a turtle or something. But I like her. I think she'll be fine."

Julie thought Alison was lucky to have Mrs. Nero as a teacher. Julie had been in Mrs. Leff's class for two hours already, and she didn't feel lucky at all. "I wish I was with you in Mrs. Nero's class," said Julie.

"Maybe your mother could have you switched," Alison said.

"Oh yeah? What could she say?" Julie asked.

"I don't know," said Alison. "She could say that . . . you have an allergy to Mrs. Leff. That her perfume makes you sneeze, or her shampoo makes you break out in tiny bumps."

"No one would believe it," said Julie. Just then, she looked up and saw that someone was standing there. It was Mr. Graham. He had come out for a drink of water too.

"Well hi, girls," he said. "You two are still inseparable, huh?"

"Yeah," said Julie. "I guess so."

"That's good," said Mr. Graham, and then he leaned over and took a drink of water. Alison and Julie just stared at him, as if he was a rock star who just happened to have wandered into the school. When he finished drinking he stood up and said, "Your know, Anna and Toby really miss you and your friends. If your new teachers don't keep you too busy with homework, maybe you'd like to come by and visit. No babysitting, no housework, just a plain old visit."

"Great!" said Julie and Alison at exactly the same second. They were so close that this kind of thing happened pretty often.

"How about Saturday afternoon?" asked Mr. Graham. "Tell Trina, Stacy, and Susan, okay?" Julie and Alison said they felt sure that everyone would be able to come. Who would want to pass up a chance to visit Mr. Graham, and his kids? "Toby and Anna really like all of you," said Mr. Graham, "and I think it's important for them to have people in their life who they know will be there at least once in a while." He paused. "It's sinking in, that their mother isn't coming back." Neither Julie nor Alison knew how to respond. "Well," said Mr. Graham, "I should be getting back to class. See you Saturday."

Alison and Julie stood watching Mr. Graham walk back to his classroom. "Boy," said Alison, "I wish there was something we could do for him. When he mentioned Toby and Anna, he seemed really sad."

Julie also wanted more than anything to find a way to help Mr. Graham and his kids, but she knew this wasn't the time to talk about it. She had to get back to her own class, or else Mrs. Leff would soon be after her, her hands on her hips, calling "Julia!" down the long stretch of hall.

# Chapter Three

That afternoon, Julie sat in the den with her mother and Dennis, playing Monopoly. When Dennis rolled the dice, he knew exactly where he was going to land on the board without having to count it out square by square, like normal people. He simply whisked his shoe-shaped marker over to where it belonged. Julie and her mother always let him be in charge of money when they played Monopoly, because he could count it out in his head like a teller at a bank. He was great with anything that had to do with numbers or science or words. But when it came to anything that had to do with human beings, he wasn't so great.

Dennis had no friends. Occasionally he invited a boy from his class to the house—another shy, shuffling kid who was really smart too—but after a while, the other kid usually dropped him. Dennis was too bossy, and if the boys did science experiments together, Dennis had to be in charge. The truth was, he was better at it than anybody else. He knew what should be done, and he had very little patience for anyone who figured things out too slowly.

Once Julie had overheard her mother talking to her father about Dennis on the phone long distance; they were talking about how smart he was. "He's really bored in school," her mother had said. "His teacher said he's so advanced that we have to be sure to keep him interested, or else he'll just tune out." Then she paused, because Julie's father was obviously saying something. "No," she replied to his question, "we don't have to worry about Julie at all. Julie will be just fine. You know Julie; she always just fits right in."

It was a compliment, *sort of,* Julie thought as she stood outside the door of her mother's bedroom, but it didn't really feel like one. It almost felt like an insult; the truth was that Julie wasn't as smart as her little brother, and everyone knew that. In a way it was kind of embarrassing. Julie was the ordinary one; she just "fit right in."

Now Julie's mother spun the dice, then counted out the squares. She landed on "Go to Jail," and Julie and Dennis let out a whoop. "Mom, you're always going to jail," Dennis said.

“There’s still hope,” said Ms. Hopwood. “I can come up from behind and take you two by storm.”

“Fat chance,” said Julie. She spun and landed on Atlantic Avenue, which she decided to buy.

“So tell me about your first day back at school,” said Ms. Hopwood. “We haven’t had a chance to really go over everything blow by blow.”

Julie shrugged. “Oh, it was okay, I guess,” she said. “Mrs. Leff is weird.”

“Weird how?” her mother asked.

Julie told her mother about the way Mrs. Leff kept talking about her old class in Kansas City. “She said those kids were *perfect,*” Julie said.

“Well, I’ve never met anybody who was truly perfect,” said Ms. Hopwood. “Maybe your teacher was just exaggerating to make a point. That’s what we writers do, anyway.”

“What do you mean?” asked Julie.

“I’ll give you an example,” said her mother. “I might write a scene in my novel in which I want to let the reader know that the Hathaways’ house is really messy.”

“Gee,” said Julie. “What a good imagination you have.”

“Very funny, Miss Sarcastic,” said her mother. “Anyway, I wouldn’t just write, ‘The house looked messy.’ That wouldn’t be very interesting to read. Instead, I go out of my way to describe several messy things in the house, and along the way I usually make it much worse than the way it is in real life. Like if Dennis takes a shower and leaves two towels on the floor, in the book I'll make sure there are *three* towels on the floor. That sort of thing."

Julie liked it when her mother told her things that writers sometimes do, especially now that she herself had begun writing in the purple journal.

"And tell me about *your* day, Dennis," Ms. Hopwood said. "Any better luck?"

Dennis shrugged too. "Not really," he said. "Mrs. Liebert is just okay. We started doing these math problems in the math book, but I knew all of them by heart, so it was pretty boring."

"Didn't I tell you not to read the fourth-grade math book over the summer?" Ms. Hopwood said. "I told you that you'd only be bored in school if you did."

"But the summer was so *boo-ooring,"* said Dennis. "And the math book was interesting, Mom. But now I already know the whole thing, and I hate having to do it again. Maybe when we're doing math, I could slip a comic book inside my math book. Nobody would ever know."

"Well, *I* would know," said Ms. Hopwood, "and I wouldn't like it."

In addition to being a genius, Dennis also had one of the biggest comic book collections in town.

If he wasn't in the basement doing a science experiment or working out math problems on his little blackboard, Dennis was lying on his bed with a copy of "The Human Sponge" in front of his face. Julie thought it was a disgusting comic; it was all about this man named Rick Doolittle, who was out of work and lived all alone since his wife and daughter had been kidnapped by villains. He was always plotting to get his family back, and to help him do this he used his amazing ability to turn himself into a sponge and absorb huge amounts of liquid, including, in one issue, the Pacific Ocean.

"I'm sure school will pick up for both of you," said Ms. Hopwood.

"It won't be like last year," Julie muttered.

"No, probably not," said her mother. "But you wouldn't want the same year twice. You're much better off with new experiences, honey."

But Julie didn't feel that way. All she wanted was to have Mr. Graham as her teacher, but for the next year, she was stuck with Mrs. Leff.

After dinner, Alison, Stacy, Susan, and Trina came over. Last year the five friends had formed a club, dedicated to helping Mr. Graham. Tonight Trina brought over a batch of cookies that her mother had baked. They were peanut butter crisps, and they were so delicious that everybody just sat eating them in silence for a few minutes, forgetting about everything but the cookies. Trina's mother, Mrs. Alberts, was famous for her chicken pot pies, but she still found time to bake for her family.

"Your mom is such a good cook," Stacy finally said, with her mouth full.

"Yeah," said Alison, "and I love seeing her on those cartons."

Mrs. Alberts's face appeared on the red-checkered cartons that her frozen pot pies came in. It was just a drawing, but it actually looked like her, including the little lines around her mouth that showed up when she smiled.

"You know," said Trina, "a lot of those people on cartons aren't even real."

"What do you mean?" Alison asked.

"Like Betty Crocker," said Trina. "They just made her up, and drew a picture of what they thought she should look like. But she doesn't even exist. She was never even born."

*"There's no Betty Crocker?"* said Alison. "You mean all those years, when I used to sit looking at her face on the back of cake mixes, and I wondered who she was and where she lived and everything, she never even existed?"

"That's right," said Julie.

"Wow," said Alison. "That seems so . . . unfair. But at least we know that Mrs. Alberts is real, and that she really does look the way she does on the carton."

"Yeah, she looks very pretty on the carton," said Julie.

"Thanks," said Trina.

"She looks like someone you'd want to spend a whole day with," Julie added, "unlike some people I could name. One person in particular."

"Are you talking about Mrs. Leff?" asked Stacy.

Julie nodded. Mrs. Leff looked very pretty too, but she was, in fact, someone you didn't want to spend the day with. She was someone whose class you couldn't wait to leave when the bell rang.

"Boy," said Susan, "it sure is a comedown after Mr. Graham."

Everyone agreed; even the girls in other sixth-grade classes. No one was as good as Mr. Graham. No one even came close.

"Mr. Graham is the best teacher in the world," said Susan. "I want him to know we still feel that way. That we haven't forgotten about him, even though we're sixth-graders now. I wish we could do something for him."

"Oh, I almost forgot," said Julie. "Here's something we can do for Mr. Graham—he invited us over to see Anna and Toby Saturday afternoon. But he doesn't want us to baby-sit, just visit. He says Anna and Toby miss us."

"That's great," said Susan, "and I really miss them too, but I'm talking about something *big* big. Visiting once in a while isn't enough."

"Maybe we should get him something," said Stacy. "A gift. So he knows we're still thinking about him."

"What do you think he'd like?" asked Trina.

"We know he likes ties," said Julie. "He wears the coolest ties of any teacher." Mr. Graham wore all kinds of ties; most were just pretty-colored patterns, but sometimes they had little pictures on them, of tiny cameras, or a city skyline.

"A tie isn't big," said Susan. "A tie is something you give somebody on Father's Day. A tie is an ordinary thing. I mean something very special."

"We could buy him one of those really big TVs," said Stacy. "Where the screen is so big that it's like being at the movies. He could watch it and he wouldn't be lonely. My cousin has one."

"Your cousin must be rich," said Susan. "Where would we get the money for that? And anyway, the kind of thing I'm thinking about isn't like a tie or a TV or anything. It has to be something incredibly special, from us to him."

"But he has everything," said Stacy. "He has a car, and a house, and a bicycle, and shoes, and ties, and a lot of books, and enough food to eat, and two kids."

"Well," said Susan, "there's one thing that he used to have, but he doesn't have anymore."

"What's that?" Trina asked.

Susan leaned closer to her friends, and in a voice that was almost a whisper, she said, "A wife."

# Chapter Four

A *wife?* Where in the world would they find Mr. Graham a wife? Julie couldn't stop thinking about Susan's idea. She thought about the subject a lot during school. Mrs. Leff would be in the middle of talking about the French and Indian War, and suddenly Julie would start to think about Mr. Graham falling in love again, or Mr. Graham getting married. She hadn't known his wife before she died; she'd only seen the picture of her that Mr. Graham brought into class. There she'd been with Anna and Toby. Now it was just Mr. Graham and Anna and Toby.

Maybe he didn't even *want* to get married again, Julie thought. That was possible. After all, five years had passed since Julie's parents got divorced, and Ms. Hopwood still hadn't even talked about getting married again. She did go out on dates once in a while; her date would show up at the house wearing a suit and the cologne that men sometimes wear that smells like pine trees. Julie's mother would be all dressed up too, and a babysitter would come over for the evening, and Julie and Dennis and the babysitter would all watch while the man opened the door for Ms. Hopwood and they walked down the front steps together. It was always very weird.

"How soon does someone have to wait before they get married a second time?" Julie asked her mother over breakfast.

"Why do you ask?" asked Julie's mother. "Does this have something to do with your father and me?"

"No. Just wondering," said Julie.

"Well, there isn't a law about it," said Ms. Hopwood. "It's probably hard for most people to make a switch from one kind of life to another."

"But how long? Julie asked. "Years? Or maybe only one year?"

"Julie!" said her mother with a little laugh. "I couldn't possibly know the answer to that. I don't even know what you're really asking. You're being very mysterious."

"Sorry," said Julie. There was no one else to ask. She couldn't very well ask Mr. Graham himself. No, Julie and her friends would have to observe Mr. Graham closely, trying to figure out whether or not he was ready to meet someone new. After all, Julie thought, people didn't get married right after they met; Mr. Graham could go out on dates with the woman they found for him, and then maybe in a year or so, or whenever he was finally ready, he could marry her.

But who was right for Mr. Graham? That was the hard part. That morning in school, when Julie met Alison at the water fountain, they discussed their plans. Once again, Alison was already waiting when Julie arrived at the fountain. She was bending over the white ledge so it looked as if she was drinking, but in fact she was only letting the jet of water shoot up and hit the place between her mouth and her nose. Did that place between the mouth and the nose have a name? Julie wondered. That was the sort of thing that Dennis always seemed to know.

"So how's Old Lady Leff?" Alison asked.

Julie giggled. Mrs. Leff certainly wasn't an old lady, but somehow the nickname seemed to fit. "She's exactly the same as yesterday," said Julie. "Not bad, not good. I just don't really like her. I don't think anyone does." As she said this, she thought about how everybody had liked Mr. Graham, even the troublemakers, like Danny Behnke and Mark Rutlin. With any other teacher, those boys would have been wild, but Mr. Graham knew how to handle them, so they liked him.

"I have a message for you from Susan," Julie said. "She wants us all to meet tomorrow after school to discuss our plans for you-know-what. We can meet regularly on Wednesdays, if everybody is free."

"Sounds good," said Alison. "It's like last year."

"Yeah, I guess in a way it is," said Julie. Last year they used to meet every Tuesday at Mr. Graham's house after school, to take care of his kids and help out around the house. Now they would be meeting on Wednesdays to figure out how to get Mr. Graham married again.

"We'll be matchmakers," said Alison. "You know, people who find people for other people to fall in love with."

"That's a job?" said Julie. "Grown-ups do it for a living?"

"Yes," said Alison.

"Wow," said Julie. It sounded like a very easy job. She didn't have any idea yet how hard a job it could be.

The first meeting of the Wednesday Night Matchmakers was held at Susan's house. She had the neatest house of any of them; you could pick through the carpet with your fingers, and you wouldn't come up with a single dog hair or human hair or even a stray piece of unknown fluff. There was never anything on any of the surfaces in the house, either: the coffee table in the living room didn't hold books or magazines, or even, as you might expect because of its name, coffee cups. It was just a shiny glass surface that no one was allowed to go near. Susan's mother was pretty nice in a nervous way; whenever Julie came over, Mrs. Moseby always glanced down at Julie's shoes to make sure she wasn't tracking any mud into the house.

Tonight at Susan's, everyone gathered upstairs in Susan's bedroom, including her little sister, Abby, who shared the room with Susan and unfortunately was allowed to be there for everything. Everyone sat on the rug in the middle of the room except for Abby, who sat cross-legged on the top bunk of the bunk beds, beneath a poster of three Siamese cats.

"I'm not listening," she announced. "So you can say anything you want."

"Yeah, right," said Susan. "You listen to everything I say."

"I do not," said Abby.

"Do too," said Susan.

Abby was only in second grade, and she really looked up to her older sister. She wanted to follow Susan everywhere and be a part of everything that she did. Because they shared a room, Abby often got her wish.

"So," said Trina, trying to start things moving, "maybe we should begin."

"You make it sound like it's an official meeting," said Stacy.

"Well, maybe it should be," said Susan. "If we're serious about it." They all agreed that they were serious. "Okay then," said Susan. "Let's get down to business. Remember last year, when we were trying to save Mr. Graham, we wrote a charter? I think we should do the same thing now."

A charter was a good idea, Julie thought. They could get their ideas down on paper. Susan went to her desk and took out a notebook and a turquoise magic marker. She had the best handwriting of any of them; it was as neat as her family's house. Everyone contributed to the writing of the charter. In perfect, tiny letters, Susan wrote down the following:

*FINDING MR. GRAHAM A WIFE:*
*THE CHARTER*

*We, the undersigned, do solimnly swear to help our dearly beloved ex-teacher, Mr. David Graham, who is all alone in the world since his wife's car skidded on a wet road last spring and she was killed. We solimnly swear to help him find a new wife (if, in fact, he is ready for such a thing!!!) Even if he is not quite ready, we solimnly swear to look around for someone for him for the future.*

*Anyway, his children will need a mother. Everyone needs a mother. All of us, the undersigned, have mothers.*

*We have talked about it and have decided that the kind of wife Mr. Graham would be most happy with would have the following trates:*

1) *Very smart. Mr. Graham is an extremely smart person, and we are sure he wouldn't be happy with anyone who wasn't like that. They wouldn't have enough in common.*
2) *Very funny. Mr. Graham likes to tell a good joke, and he enjoys people who can keep up with his sense of humor. The second Mrs. Graham would have to be able to tell jokes and make him laugh.*
3) *Very nice. Mr. Graham is always kind. Even when he does lose his temper he always tries to make it up to the person he's lost his temper at. Also, he is never nasty or mean or unfair.*
4) *Very pretty. Mr. Graham is very handsome, and he has really clean red hair and a great mustache. Plus, his clothes are really cool for a teacher. Mr. Graham likes to look good. His wife was very pretty too, so I'm sure if he fell in*

*love again she would have to be pretty. Not like a movie star or anything, but nice to look at.*

*Those are the only things that a wife for Mr. Graham would have to have. Other than that, she can be whoever she is, as long as he loves her and his children love her. Last year our job was to make Mr. Graham happy by the end of the school year. This year we, the undersigned, are sincerely committed to introducing Mr. Graham to a woman as soon as possible. It is a very big job, but we plan to complete it successfully, OR ELSE.*

*Yours very truly,*

*Susan Moseby*
*(secretary)*
*Trina Alberts*
*Julie Hopwood*
*Stacy Geller*
*Alison Spaeth*

Everyone signed her name with Susan's magic marker, just like the year before. It felt very familiar, sitting and signing a piece of paper about Mr. Graham.

"It's very important that Mr. Graham never find out about this," said Alison. "I have a feeling that he'd get very mad if he knew. He wouldn't want us doing this."

"You mean, interfering," said Julie.

"Whatever you want to call it," said Alison.

"I agree," said Susan. "So we're all sworn to secrecy. This idea must never leave the room."

Now they needed to figure out a way to find a wife for Mr. Graham. You couldn't just walk up and down the streets of Iowa City trying to find one. You had to have a plan.

"I don't know anyone who has all those qualities that we wrote in the Charter," said Julie. "I mean, we don't even know anyone who's the right age."

But suddenly Trina looked up. She had a special look in her eyes; if she was a cartoon character, there would have been a light bulb shining over her head. "Oh yes we do," she said. "Why didn't we think of this? We know somebody who's perfect for Mr. Graham. Somebody who's nice, and pretty, and smart, and funny, and not married, and besides, one of us knows her very well."

"Who?" asked Stacy. "Who?"

Trina turned and looked straight at Julie. "Julie's mother," she said. "Ms. Hopwood!"

Julie just stared. Everyone else was saying things like, "Yeah," or "What a great idea!" But Julie couldn't say a word. She just sat there, perfectly still. It had never occurred to her to fix Mr.

Graham up with her mother. Probably if she had to make a list of all the people in the world who would be right for Mr. Graham, she could have sat there all day without ever coming up with her own mother.

"I don't know," Julie said. "I don't think so."

"Why not?" pressed Susan. "Then Mr. Graham could be your . . . father."

"I already have a father," said Julie.

"I mean your stepfather," said Susan. "You know."

Julie wasn't enjoying this conversation one bit. She ran her hand nervously through the rug. She couldn't tell her friends that she didn't want her mother to go out on a date with Mr. Graham. She loved Mr. Graham, which everybody knew, of course, except nobody thought it would bother her if her mother was in love with Mr. Graham too. But it did. Was it so wrong to want to keep these things separate? She loved both Mr. Graham and her mother, but in different ways. She didn't want the two of them to love each other.

She pictured Mr. Graham taking her mother on a date, coming to the door and ringing the bell, then stepping inside. Julie and Dennis would be sitting there with the baby-sitter, Connie, who was seventeen and did nothing but talk on the phone all night to her dumb boyfriend, Fred, and eat the Bar-b-q potato chips that Ms. Hopwood bought specially for her. Mr. Graham would think of Julie as someone who needed a baby-sitter, even though she herself had baby-sat for Anna and Toby the year before. Mr. Graham would think she was a baby. It would be very embarrassing.

There he would be, with his red mustache and a beautiful tie, and Ms. Hopwood would have on a pretty skirt and lipstick, and they would walk out the door together. It was a terrible, terrible thought. "No," said Julie. "It won't work."

"Well, why not?" asked Stacy.

"Because . . . because . . . my mother already has a boyfriend," she said. As soon as the words were out of Julie's mouth, she had no idea of where they had come from. It was a lie. Her mother didn't have a boyfriend. Everyone knew that. Her friends looked at her in surprise.

"You never told us that," said Trina.

Alison stared at Julie. They were best friends, and there was a look of hurt in her eyes, as though she couldn't understand why Julie hadn't talked to her about this.

"Well, my mother didn't want me to tell anyone," said Julie. "It's supposed to be a secret."

Suddenly Abby leaned over the side of the bed. "What's a secret?" she asked.

*"Abby!"* Susan shrieked. "Go away!"

Everyone turned back to Julie. "So," said Susan, "can you tell us about him?"

"What do you want to know?" Julie asked. She was really in over her head now.

"Well," said Alison, "you could start with his name."

# Chapter Five

Julie stared at the poster of three cats on Susan's wall. The poster suddenly gave her an idea. *Cats,* she thought. *Katz*. "His name is Mr. Katz," she said. "Michael Katz."

"What does he do?" asked Susan.

"He's a . . . writer. Like my mother," said Julie.

"That's so neat," said Trina. "Are they in love?"

"Yes," said Julie. "Definitely."

"So how did they meet?" Alison asked.

Julie closed her eyes for a second and actually pictured this made-up Michael Katz. In her mind, he had dark brown hair and wore nice, soft sweaters. "They met at a lecture. It was all writers there. It was a couple of summers ago, but they wrote letters to each other."

"Then he doesn't live around here?" Stacy asked.

"No," said Julie. "He lives in New York City."

"But how often do they get to see each other?" Trina asked.

"Oh, not very often," said Julie. "They talk on the phone a lot, and they still write letters. But they're very, very much in love."

As she spoke, it was as though she was telling the truth. She really pictured her mother and this man, Michael Katz, talking to each other on the phone late at night, whispering the kinds of things that people did when they were in love.

"Do you think they'll get married?" Stacy asked.

"Yes," said Julie. "But not right away. They want to wait."

"Well," said Susan, "then I guess you're right, we can't fix your mother up with Mr. Graham."

So the subject was closed. Julie felt her face burning a little; she couldn't remember the last time she had told such a big lie. It felt very strange. And to lie to Alison, her best friend in the world—well, that was even stranger. But she simply didn't want her mother to fall in love with Mr. Graham. That would have been the strangest thing of all.

That night when Julie was up in her own bedroom doing the dumb, boring homework that Mrs. Leff had assigned ("Write a one-page essay describing a day in the life of a Colonial family"), the telephone rang and Ms. Hopwood answered it. She was on the phone for a long time, and she even closed her bedroom door so that Julie and Dennis couldn't hear. After a while, Dennis wandered into Julie's room without knocking. He did this a lot lately, and it drove Julie crazy.

"Who's Mom talking to?" Dennis asked.

"How should I know?" said Julie.

"Well, she's been on a long time," said Dennis, and he flopped himself down on the foot of Julie's bed.

"Don't you have homework?" she asked.

"I did it already," said Dennis. "It took me like two minutes."

Julie couldn't stand how quickly Dennis did everything. He could do his homework while listening to the radio, and he would still get a good grade. But Julie spent forever on her homework. Nothing came easily to her. It wasn't that she was a bad student, but compared to Dennis she felt really dumb. She looked down at the page she was trying to write, about Colonial life. Already there were dozens of faint pink marks where she had erased a word she had written. The desktop was covered with eraser crumbs too. Julie had a lot of trouble trying to write, which was really a surprise, because her mother was such a good writer. Sometimes, when Julie felt as though she had no talent, she wondered if she were adopted. She had read a book about that: a girl discovers she's adopted when her class in school learns about genetics. Genetics is all about the kinds of things you inherit from your parents. In this book, the teacher had told the class that two blue-eyed parents could never have a brown-eyed child. But the girl in the book had brown eyes, and her parents had blue. So she realized that she was adopted, even though her parents had kept it a secret from her.

But Julie looked very much like both of her parents; she had her father's sharp chin and small nose, and her mother's dark blonde curls. There was no way in the world that she had been adopted; but why wasn't she talented like everyone else in her family? Her father was a very good lawyer, and everyone always complimented him on his legal briefs, which were the papers that lawyers wrote about the cases they were working on. Her mother was such a good writer that people wrote her fan letters about her books all the time. She received letters from people she had never met, saying how much they loved the Hathaway family, and how real they seemed. And Dennis, of course, was good at everything. But Julie didn't have anything about her that really made her stand out.

Now Ms. Hopwood appeared in the doorway of Julie's room. She had a secretive expression on her face. Julie wondered who she had been talking to. "Who was on the phone?" she asked her mother.

"Oh, just a personal matter," said her mother. And that was all she would say.

Later that night, Julie's mother called Julie's father in Los Angeles. First Julie and Dennis spoke to him, each of them trying to grab the telephone from the other. Finally they got on separate extensions and talked to him at the same time.

"Dad," said Dennis, "I'm reading a book about magnetic fields. It's really cool."

"That's great," said Mr. Hopwood. "I'm sure it's very interesting." He paused. "How about you, Julie? Are you doing anything interesting with yourself?"

She wanted to tell her father about Mr. Graham. She wanted to ask him about finding Mr. Graham a wife, but she didn't. She had never talked to her father about anything like that. "Not really," she answered. "Just getting used to school. You know."

"Well, I hope it's a great year," said Mr. Hopwood. "Could you put your mother back on? And remember, I really miss you guys."

"We miss you too, Dad," said Julie, and she meant it.

A while later, when Julie was in bed, she heard her mother still talking to her father on the phone across the hall. She was talking in a quiet voice, but Julie strained to listen. She heard her mother say, "Yes, Dan, I know, but here's the situation . . ." What were they talking about? Julie wondered. It sounded pretty interesting.

But although Julie tried hard to listen, the words faded out from time to time. After a while, she felt herself drifting off. Finally she shut off the bedside light and fell asleep. Soon she was having a long dream about cats, and the next thing she knew, the dream was over, and the night was over, and the morning was already in motion. Downstairs, she could hear her mother rummaging through the pots, and the kitchen radio playing the local news. Julie forgot all about her mother's talk with her father. Her thoughts turned instead to school.

That day in class, Mrs. Leff had the kids read their homework assignments aloud. One by one, they stood up and read about what it was like to live in Colonial times. First Adam Lewin read. For a boy, he was pretty nice. He was loud, but not mean. The year before, he had been the first person in Mr. Graham's class to have a co-ed birthday party. Adam was small and had dark hair in bangs. Already a couple of girls said that he was "cute." "Cute" or "gross" were the only two words that girls used to describe boys. Adam stood and read his assignment in a loud voice.

He was having a good time, really getting into it. "This is what life was like in Colonial times," he began. "It was nothing like the way it is now. If you got bored, forget about watching TV, because TV did not exist! Neither did video games!" A couple of kids giggled. Suddenly Mrs. Leff interrupted Adam.

"We can hear you just fine," she said. "You don't need to shout, Adam."

Adam stopped, surprised. "Okay," he said, and he continued to read the rest of it in a quiet, dull voice. When he was done, she just said, "Thank you." Then she called on Ilene Bray, a very shy girl whom no one knew very well. When Ilene finished reading, Mrs. Leff said "Thank you," in exactly the same way she'd said it to Adam. It was as though she didn't want to single anybody out, or make anybody feel bad. Or good.

She didn't seem wild about anybody's homework assignment, and her face had a pinched expression on it as she sat behind her desk listening. She called on Julie, and Julie stood up at the front of the room and began to read. She looked over at Mrs. Leff, but the teacher's face didn't show real interest or enthusiasm or *anything*. Mrs. Leff could have been daydreaming, or making up a shopping list in her head, for all Julie knew. She thought about last year, and the way Mr. Graham would perch on the edge of his desk when kids stood up to read. It was as though he were watching a really exciting movie and didn't want to miss a word of it.

When Julie was done, she waited for her "thank you," then sat back down. Finally all the kids had read, even Danny Behnke, who had written a really bad, really short assignment that sounded as if a third-grader wrote it. But most of the assignments had been pretty good, Julie thought. Now Mrs. Leff had her hands folded on her desk. "Class," she said, "I have to tell you something. Some of your assignments were good, and others were less than good. But I don't have the feeling that anybody really spent too long on his or her assignment. Nobody really went all out."

Everyone just sat and looked at her. Nobody knew what to say. Julie thought she had put a lot of time into her homework. Was she supposed to spend all day on it? No teacher had ever asked them to do that before. Mr. Graham had never spoken to his class like this. If he felt they hadn't done a good job on something, he said said, "Come on. You know this isn't your best work. Let's take another crack at it tomorrow, okay?" But Mrs. Leff was just making everyone squirm a little in their seats.

"My class in Kansas City did this same assignment," she continued, "and one girl came to class in *full Colonial dress,* with a butter churn that she had built at home with the help of her father! It was truly wonderful." Mrs. Leff smiled at the memory.

Full Colonial dress! It would never have occurred to Julie to do something like that for a simple homework assignment. Julie pictured that girl sitting in front of Mrs. Leff's classroom, her hand pumping up and down on her homemade butter churn. But Julie had the feeling that even if she had come into class with an entire skit rehearsed, complete with music and slides and charts, Mrs. Leff still wouldn't have thought it was as good as her students in Kansas. Julie didn't even know those kids, but she secretly hated them anyway.

She looked around the room at Susan and Adam Lewin and Tracy Frost, and even at Danny Behnke, who thought he was so tough and cool. They were an okay class, she realized. If only Mrs. Leff thought so too. But so far, Mrs. Leff had nothing good to say about them.

At 11:19, the time she and Alison had agreed on for today, Julie was the first to arrive at the water fountain. She bent over to drink, and within a few seconds, Alison had arrived. "I couldn't wait to get out of there," said Julie. "Mrs. Leff keeps talking about her other class and how great they were. I'm starting to feel like something's wrong with *our* class. No matter what we do, we're not good enough."

"That's ridiculous," said Alison. "You shouldn't let her make you feel that way. You're a great class. I mean, except for Danny Behnke, of course."

"Well, we'll never be as good as the kids in Kansas City," said Julie.

"Hey, Jule?" Alison said. "Can I ask you something?"

"Sure," said Julie.

Alison looked very uncomfortable. "It's about your mom and her boyfriend, Mr. Katz."

"What about them?" Julie asked nervously.

"Well, how come you never told me about it before?" asked Alison. "I'm your best friend in the world, right?"

"Of course you are!" said Julie. "It isn't that. I told you . . . my mom didn't want me saying anything. I'm really sorry. Are you angry with me?"

Alison thought about it. "No, I guess not," she said. "It's just the first time that you haven't told me something."

"Well, now I *have* told you," said Julie, and Alison nodded. Things would be fine between them. Julie felt a little wave of relief. But then she remembered that she was lying to Alison, her best friend in the world. This was much worse than if her mother actually had a boyfriend and she hadn't told Alison about him. This was a great big lie. How could she lie to her best friend? For a moment, there at the water fountain, Julie almost blurted out the truth about her mother. This was the time to do it, right now, when it was just the two of them. Alison would be really mad, but it would only last a day or two, and then they could make up. Julie decided that this was the thing to do—she had to tell Alison the truth.

She took a deep breath. "Hey, Al?" she said, but just then a voice boomed down the hall.

*"Julia Hopwood!"* it called.

Julie looked up. Way down at the end of the hall was Mrs. Leff. She had her hands on her hips. She just stood there, looking very pretty but also very angry. "Are you ever planning on coming back into class, Julia?" asked Mrs. Leff. "This must have been one incredibly long drink of water!"

"Sorry," called Julie. She turned to Alison. "I've got to go," she said.

*"Julia?"* said Alison. "She calls you Julia?"

"Yeah," said Julie. She rolled her eyes.

"Well, good luck," said Alison. "I'll see you at lunch."

As Julie slowly walked down the hall toward her teacher, she wondered to herself whether the kids in Kansas City ever used the water fountain.

They were probably like camels, who could trudge through the desert for weeks without once needing to stop for water. Now Julie trudged down the long, glistening hall.

She passed by Mr. Graham's classroom. Inside, his students were sitting in a big circle, and he was on the floor in the middle, doing some kind of experiment that seemed to involve a lit candle and a Slinky. It was painful for her to watch this; it was like a mirage right in the middle of the desert. She had read a book once that explained what a mirage was; when people are out in the desert sun for too long, they sometimes start to see things that aren't there—wonderful things, like entire cities in the distance, or a beautiful blue lake. Seeing Mr. Graham in his classroom was like that; it was a sight that seemed so wonderful and perfect, but which she knew she could never have again.

At the end of the hall, Mrs. Leff was waiting.

# Chapter Six

*Dear Journal,*

*So much has happened since I wrote last. One night my mother got a telephone call from someone, and Dennis and I didn't know who it was. But the next night over dinner, my mother said there was something she wanted to talk about. It was about Dennis, she said, but she wanted me to hear it as well. That mystery telephone call, she said, came from the psychologist at our elementary school, Dr. Glenn. Dr. Glenn said that she felt that Dennis was so far beyond the rest of his class that he was much too bored, and he made the other kids feel a little slow. Even though my mother had already said she didn't want Dennis to skip a grade, Dr. Glenn asked my mother to think about it. So that night my mother called my father and they had a long talk. The next day, my mother met with Dr. Glenn, and then she and my father talked again, and this time they decided that it was okay to let Dennis skip a grade and move into a new class.*

*Well, Journal, I know that none of this sounds all that fascinating, but there's one important thing that I haven't mentioned: On Monday my brother moved into his new fifth-grade class. And do you know who his teacher is? That's right:* Mr. Graham.

*I just can't believe it! It's bad enough that* I *don't have Mr. Graham as a teacher anymore, and that I had to prevent my friends from fixing him up with my mother. But this is absolutely the worst of all! My obnoxious little brother is seeing Mr. Graham every day and listening to him talk about things like the solar system, and how the sandwich got invented by someone named the Earl of Sandwich. And meanwhile, down the hall, I'm sitting and* not *listening to Mrs. Leff talk about her wonderful students in Kansas. It just isn't fair. I can't believe that my mother and father allowed Dennis to switch to Mr. Graham's class. Don't they have any feelings at all?*

*This year is really turning out to be a disaster. Mrs. Leff has no sense of humor. Whenever someone tells a joke, she sort of squints her eyes and looks confused. And she always insists that the classroom be really quiet. She likes to put her finger to her lips and say, "Shhhh!" whenever anybody says anything in an excited voice. I wonder if she has any kids at home, and if she shushes them whenever they're having fun.*

On Saturday afternoon, Julie and her friends biked over to Coralville to Mr. Graham's house. They had seen his children in August, and even though not too much time had passed, Anna and Toby looked different: taller, stronger, frecklier. Anna threw her arms around each of the girls. "I learned a new song in school!' she said before anyone had even taken off a jacket. "It goes like this!" And then she sang a song about a purple horse. Toby was spinning in a circle, then standing still and giggling as the room spun around before his eyes. It felt so good to be here again, to be playing with Anna and Toby.

At the end of the afternoon, when Toby looked ready to collapse, and Anna had gone into the den to watch her favorite TV show, Mr. Graham walked the girls out to the driveway, where their bicycles were parked. "I'm really glad you came," he said to the group. "It means a lot to the kids."

"They're really great," said Stacy.

"Yeah," agreed Mr. Graham. "And pretty active too, wouldn't you say?"

"It must be hard running all over the place after them," said Susan.

"Well, Mrs. Fine next door helps out during the week," said Mr. Graham. "But on weekends they're all mine. It's great, but it *is* exhausting, I'll admit."

Everyone said good-bye and rode off, leaving the Graham family to fend for themselves. The girls would see Mr. Graham in the halls at school, and maybe occasionally on a Saturday afternoon, if he invited them to visit his kids, but that was it. And meanwhile, as if to drive Julie crazy, her brother Dennis could talk about nothing but Mr. Graham.

After his first day in Mr. Graham's class, Dennis came home with a big smile on his face. He threw down his knapsack and said, "Mr. Graham's teaching us the ocarina!" The ocarina was a musical instrument that Julie had learned to play when she was in Mr. Graham's class. But the way Dennis acted, Julie thought, you'd think he was the first person in the world to ever play one. You'd think he'd *invented* the ocarina.

Over dinner, Dennis continued to talk about Mr. Graham. He wound up a big forkful of spaghetti and said, "I can see why you liked him so much, Julie. He's really a cool guy. And you know what? I'm not bored anymore."

"That's wonderful," said Ms. Hopwood. "It's nice to see a satisfied customer."

Julie looked down at her plate of spaghetti. Her mother was in a good mood because she'd had a good day writing her novel, and her brother was in a good mood because he was in Mr. Graham's class. Julie was the only one who was in a bad mood.

The only thing that seemed like any fun at all was the idea of finding Mr. Graham a wife. But where would they find one? Julie wondered. She thought about the way she had told her friends that her mother had met Mr. Katz. She said that they had met at a conference for writers. She didn't know where she had come up with that idea, but for some reason she could picture the whole thing, and so she began to write it down in her journal:

*Mom and Mr. Katz: How They Met*

*My mom is at a conference in New York City. There is a big room filled with writers. She is very bored and falls asleep, and as she's asleep her hand opens and her purse thuds to the ground. So this nice guy with wavy brown hair and a nice sweater sitting behind her reaches forward and taps her shoulder. Mom wakes up with a jolt. She has no idea of where she is.*

*"Excuse me," says wavy brown hair. "I think you dropped your purse."*

*Mom is grateful to him. After the lecture, as she's leaving the room, she stops and thanks him. He tells her his name is Mr. Katz. He's a widower. His wife died a long time ago, and they didn't have any children. After she died, his best friend bought him two cats—both as a joke, because of his name, and also to keep him company. Mom says she really likes cats, although she's allergic to them. Mr. Katz laughs and says in that case, they can never get married, because his cats are like his children and he would never give them up. He even gave them real human names: Anthony and Gwendolyn.*

*By the time the weekend ends, Mom is madly in love with him. He goes with her to the airport. "Oh, Mr. Katz," she says, "I've never met a man like you. Since my husband and I got divorced, I've been so lonely. But you make me laugh and you make me feel good. I love being with you. I will miss you when you're gone."*

*"Please," he says, "call me Michael."*

*And then they kiss. As she breaks away*

*from him and runs up the ramp to catch her airplane, there are tears in her eyes.*

*The End*

How could Julie and her friends find a real person for Mr. Graham to fall in love with, not just a made-up one? Maybe, Julie thought, they should really start to look. So a week later, on the following Saturday morning, the girls arranged to meet at the Down Street Mall, a place where they liked to spend time. Sometimes they would spend the entire day at the mall, just going from store to store, trying on clothes, having lunch, going to a movie at the sixplex, getting free samples of perfume that the ladies handed out at the foot of the escalator in Bruckner's, the big department store.

Today the girls gathered outside Bruckner's. They decided they would split up and start looking for possible wives for Mr. Graham. Trina and Susan went to the shoe department, Stacy headed over to cosmetics, and Alison and Julie went up to women's clothing. They arranged to meet back at the entrance of the store in an hour, each with the name and phone number of a date for Mr. Graham in hand.

Julie stood in the women's clothing department, pretending to look through a rack of blouses, while Alison stood beside her, giggling a little. "What do you think of this one, *Philomena?"* Alison asked in a loud voice, holding out a bright pink blouse that cost $90.

"Well, it's a little loud for my taste, *Doreen,"* said Julie, and then they both cracked up.

A saleswoman wandered by and raised an eyebrow at them. "Can I help you girls with something?" she asked.

"No thanks," said Alison. "We're browsing." And then they both cracked up again. The woman walked away.

The department was pretty quiet. There was a young mother shopping with her baby in a stroller; she was pretty, but Julie figured she was already married and wouldn't go out on a date with Mr. Graham. There was another woman looking through dresses, but she was a lot older than Mr. Graham. And then Julie saw someone else.

This one had blonde hair that was tied back off her face, and there were sunglasses perched on top of her head. She was wearing a pretty yellow outfit, and even though she wasn't smiling right now, she looked as though she smiled a lot. She was standing in front of a rack of blazers, and she kept pulling them out and squinting at them to see if she wanted to try them on. Julie took a deep breath and then worked up the courage to speak. "That one looks nice," she said.

The woman looked up. "Oh, you think so?" she asked.

"Yes," said Julie. "I bet it will look good on you."

"Oh, I don't know," said the woman. "You don't think it's . . . too young?"

"Oh no," said Julie. "I mean, that depends on how old you are, I guess."

"I'm thirty-five," the woman said.

Thirty-five! That was the perfect age for Mr. Graham! Julie was getting excited now. Alison kept nodding and mouthing words from the other side of the rack. The woman tried on the jacket, and it did look great.

"Do you think I should get it?" she asked.

"Yes, definitely," said Julie.

"Well, thanks for all your help," said the woman. "You've been a great shopper's assistant."

She started to walk to the cash register to pay for the jacket. Alison came rushing up to Julie and pulled her behind the discount rack. "She's perfect!" Alison hissed. "Absolutely perfect!"

"But we don't know anything about her yet," said Julie. "We don't even know her name."

"That's easy enough," said Alison. "She's probably going to pay for the jacket with a credit card. You can kind of stand next to her and look over her shoulder. And then you can start chatting, and you can tell her about Mr. Graham."

Julie was very nervous, but she thought about poor Mr. Graham raising Toby and Anna all by himself. He shouldn't have to do that alone, she thought. He should have a wife. So Julie took another deep breath and walked over to the counter. The blonde woman's jacket was already being rung up and folded into a box with tissue paper. The saleswoman behind the counter—the same one who had raised her eyebrow at Julie—was holding the credit card. She pressed it into one of those little credit-card machines and pushed the lever across. She was chatting as she worked.

"It's been pretty quiet around here so far," she was saying. "Couple of months and it will get real busy, what with Christmas and all."

Christmas! It was only September. Julie stood at the counter beside the blonde woman, and tried to join in the conversation somehow. "Yes, Christmas is a busy time," Julie suddenly said, as though the two women had been talking to her. The women looked up in surprise.

"What's that, dear?" asked the saleswoman.

"Christmas," Julie mumbled. "You know."

They both looked a little puzzled, and Julie just wanted to disappear, she felt so embarrassed. The saleswoman took the credit card out of the machine and handed it back to the blonde woman. "Here you go, Miss Coyle," she said.

*Miss* Coyle! So she wasn't married. This was starting to look very promising. Julie watched while the saleswoman handed Miss Coyle her package. She took it under her arm, said "Thank you," and started to walk away from the counter. Julie didn't know what to do. Alison came up beside her and whispered that they should follow the woman. So they did. They stayed six feet behind her and trailed her as she walked to the Down escalator. Miss Coyle got on and then Julie and Alison waited several agonizing seconds before getting on it too. They stood quietly behind her, and when she got off they were still on the escalator and had a good view of where she was heading. She walked across the main floor of Bruckner's and went straight to the cosmetics counter.

Stacy was right there, pretending to be interested in lipsticks, even though none of the girls were allowed to wear lipstick yet. Stacy saw Julie and Alison and started to say hi, but they wildly shushed her, their fingers to their lips. Alison pointed toward Miss Coyle, and Stacy understood. Alison and Julie hung back, partially hiding behind a big display called What Is Your Skin Type? It had all sorts of little windows and slots and buttons on it, and it was designed to look like a computer. If you answered all the questions and slid all the latches into the right place, it was supposed to tell you what kind of soap and makeup you should use. Alison started reading what it said, and answering the questions about her own skin. She was getting very involved in it.

"Alison!" Julie hissed. "We're supposed to be spying!"

"Sorry," said Alison.

They watched as Miss Coyle picked up a little bottle of perfume and sprayed some onto her wrist. Then she lifted her wrist and sniffed it. She put the bottle down. "How much is this?" she asked the saleswoman.

"Twenty-five dollars," the saleswoman answered. "But it comes with a free bottle of bath oil too."

"I'll take it," said Miss Coyle. She took out her charge card again and paid for the perfume.

How were they supposed to say anything to her? The only way would be for Julie to go up to her and say, "Oh, hi, it's you again! That's a great perfume you're wearing. What is it?" And maybe pretty soon they'd be having a real conversation, and Julie would tell her all about Mr. Graham. But she just couldn't do it. She stayed frozen behind the skin-type computer.

"Come on, Julie," whispered Alison. "Here's your chance."

But before Julie had time to do anything, she felt a hand on her arm. It was Miss Coyle. She was standing right there and looking at Julie, who suddenly had to go to the bathroom in the worst way. "All right," said Miss Coyle in a low voice. "I know you've been following me. And I'd like an explanation."

# Chapter Seven

Julie found herself staring straight into the eyes of Miss Coyle. She swallowed hard. Beside her, Alison was looking terrified, as though they'd been caught shoplifting.

"Uh, it's not what you think," Julie said to Miss Coyle, even though she had no idea of what Miss Coyle really did think. Julie began to explain the story about finding Mr. Graham a date. "He's the greatest teacher in the world," Julie said. "And he's very cute too. He's about your age. I think you'd like him a lot. That's all I was doing—trying to find a way to see if you wanted to go out with Mr. Graham."

Miss Coyle had let go of Julie's arm by now, and she was smiling a little. "Well, that's very sweet," she said. "But I don't think my boyfriend would think it was such a good idea."

"Your *boyfriend?*" said Julie.

"Yes," said Miss Coyle. "His name is Dan, and we're planning on getting married this summer."

"Oh," said Julie. "That's too bad."

Miss Coyle laughed. "Some people would say congratulations."

"Sorry," said Julie. "Congratulations. It's just too bad for Mr. Graham."

A little while later, the girls all met by the entrance of the store for lunch. They compared notes, and found that no one had discovered anyone perfect for Mr. Graham. Trina and Susan had met a nice woman named Ingrid, but she spoke almost no English, and was planning on moving back to Norway in the fall. Stacy kept finding women who already wore wedding rings.

"How do adults meet each other?" asked Julie over hot dogs at Frank's Footlong.

"At parties," said Susan. "Or they're introduced by friends."

"Or else," said Trina, "they put a personal ad in the newspaper." Everybody perked up.

"You know," said Susan, "the *Crier* accepts free ads." The *Crier* was the local shoppers' newspaper. "And their storefront is right here in the mall," Susan went on. "I know because my mother put in an ad last year to sell our dining room furniture."

"That means we could write an ad right now," said Stacy, "and drop it off today."

All the girls grew excited, and quickly finished their hot dogs. When everybody was through, and they had wiped the mustard and sauerkraut from the tabletop, Julie took out her handbag. Inside was her journal, and she ripped a piece of paper out of it and they all joined in writing an ad. This is what they came up with:

> Young Widower Looking for a Nice, Pretty Woman. Must Like Children, Music, and Corny Jokes. Who Knows? Maybe It Will Lead to Love . . .

"Perfect!" squealed Alison when they had finished. "I bet that will bring a lot of responses." They walked over to the *Crier* storefront, which was located between two shops, Betty's Dresses for Big Women, and the Popcorn Shack, which featured popcorn in twenty different flavors, including watermelon. There was no one in the *Crier* office except for a bald man behind the counter. The girls had decided that Susan would be in charge. She took the piece of paper and walked right up to the man. Everyone else stayed a couple feet behind her.

"Excuse me, sir," said Susan. "I'd like to place an ad."

"Okay," said the bald man. "Let's have a look."

She handed him the piece of paper and he read it. Then he glanced up at the group of girls. "Which one of you is the widower?" he asked. Everybody started to giggle.

"It's for a friend," said Stacy. "He asked us to drop it off. He had to stay home and take care of his children. He's all alone."

"Well, all right," said the bald man. He explained the way the *Crier*'s personal ads worked: each ad was assigned a number—in their case it was #3468. The ad would run the following Saturday. A week after that, they could stop by the *Crier* office and ask if there had been any replies for #3468. If there were, they would be handed the letters.

"Do you think we—I mean, *he*—will get any answers?" Julie asked.

The man shrugged. "Can't say," he said. "You can never tell whether a letter will spark the attention of other people, or whether it will just lie there gathering dust."

Throughout the week, Julie could think of little else but the personal ad. In school, her class was doing something called "Quiet Time," which Mrs. Leff had invented. For an hour every day, the students sat at their desks and wrote in their workbooks, while Mrs. Leff sat up front at her desk and corrected papers. After only ten minutes, kids started twitching in their seats and asking if they could go to the bathroom or get a drink of water.

One day during Quiet Time, Julie's foot fell asleep. She had been doing phonics in her workbook when she realized that her entire left foot felt numb. She banged it against the leg of her chair, and it stung in that way that her mother called pins and needles. She just had to walk on it, or else it would get worse. Julie raised her hand. But Mrs. Leff was looking down at the papers she was correcting. How could Julie get her attention without saying anything? If she called out Mrs. Leff's name, that would be speaking out of turn, and Mrs. Leff didn't like that. So instead she coughed. She began to cough and cough, as though she had a terrible cold, and eventually Mrs. Leff looked up from her work.

"Are you all right, Julia?" she asked.

"It's my foot," said Julie. "It fell asleep." Danny Behnke made a snoring sound. "Can I go out in the hall and walk around on it?" Julie asked.

"Well, all right, but come back right away," said Mrs. Leff. "Quiet Time is very important, you know."

Julie limped out of the classroom. Her mother was right; she felt as though little pins and needles were being stuck all over her foot. She looked up as she limped and saw Mr. Graham coming down the hall. He was carrying a stapler, and wearing a tie that had little black and white panda bears on it. Julie felt suddenly very embarrassed and happy all at once; that was the way she often felt when she saw Mr. Graham.

"Well, hi, Julie," he said. "Are you okay?"

"I'm fine, Mr. Graham," she said.

"You're limping. Did you sprain your ankle?" he asked.

"No," she said. "My foot fell asleep."

"Oh," he said. "That happens to me sometimes when I'm teaching. I have a cure for it. You take your hand and you run it all over your foot really hard, like you were giving it a massage. And then in a few minutes your foot won't be asleep anymore. It'll be wide awake."

She tried Mr. Graham's method, and pretty soon her foot felt fine. She smiled up at him. "Thanks a lot," she said.

"Oh, you're very welcome," said Mr. Graham. "Well, I'd better go back to my class. I went to get refills for my stapler, and by now they're probably climbing the walls."

"Uh, Mr. Graham?" said Julie suddenly.

"Yes?" he asked.

Julie didn't know exactly what she wanted to say. She wanted to tell him everything all at once: how disappointing Mrs. Leff was, how jealous Julie was of her brother Dennis, because he was in Mr. Graham's class, how she and her friends were busy trying to find him a wife. But when she opened her mouth to speak, all she said was, "I just want to let you know that I really miss Anna and Toby."

Mr. Graham smiled at her. "Well, they miss you too," he said. "They ask about you girls all the time. Maybe you'd like to stop by and visit again soon."

"That would be great," said Julie.

"Well, bye," said Mr. Graham. "I'm going to go tame my wild fifth-grade animals. Your little brother included." He waved and walked away. As she watched him go, she wished there was something she could say that would keep him there. He walked back into his classroom, and it was all she could do to keep from following him in.

That night at dinner, Julie tried to quiz her brother Dennis on Mr. Graham. Her mother had brought in Chinese food and they were sitting around the table helping themselves to fried rice and chicken with peanuts. Julie loved Chinese food; it was much better than her mother's cooking. She picked up her chopsticks and tried to use them, but the food just fell off in a big lump.

"Here's how you use them," said Dennis. "You

slide them between your fingers like this, and then they can move very easily."

How did he know so much? It always amazed her. Sometimes it seemed that Dennis was born knowing everything. "So, how's Mr. Graham?" she asked, managing to keep a few grains of rice sticking to the side of one of the chopsticks.

"Fine," said Dennis. "He taught us a cool song today. It goes like this: 'We're going on a bear hunt/We're going on a bear hunt. . . .' "

"I already know that song," said Julie impatiently. "He taught it to us last year. I know he's a great teacher. But how does he *seem* to you? You know, like as a person?"

Dennis just blinked at her. "As a *person?*" he said, as though it had never occurred to him that Mr. Graham was actually human.

"Yes," said Julie. "Does he seem happy, or sad, or depressed, or lonely, or what? His wife died last year, you know."

"Yes, I *know,*" said Dennis. "You've only talked about it like a million times, Julie."

"Well?" asked Julie. "How does he seem?"

"I don't know," said Dennis, shrugging. "He seems like . . . like Mr. Graham. The same as always."

Dennis might know all the facts that were in the encyclopedia, Julie thought, but he didn't seem to know anything about feelings. He was in his own world half the time, and probably wouldn't notice if Mr. Graham was lonely or exhausted.

"Why are you so concerned about Mr. Graham?" asked Julie's mother.

"I just wonder if he's doing okay," said Julie. "He's all alone."

"Well, he's got his kids," said Ms. Hopwood. "That counts for something, doesn't it? I don't think of myself as all alone, you know. Even though Dad and I are divorced, I still feel like you and Dennis and I are a family."

But it had to be hard sometimes, Julie knew. She saw that look in her mother's eyes once in a while; a faraway expression that meant she wished there were another adult around to talk to. Mr. Graham probably got that same expression too, when he was sitting at the dinner table with Anna and Toby, and his wife wasn't there.

The more Julie thought about Mr. Graham, the more she wanted to help him. If she and her friends found Mr. Graham a wife, he would be grateful to them forever. He and his new wife would invite the girls over to their house to thank them.

The new Mrs. Graham would answer the door, and Mr. Graham would be standing right behind her, his hands on her shoulders. "Girls," he would say, "you introduced me to this wonderful lady, and now she has become my wife. You girls have made me happier than I have been in a long time. I never thought I would get over the death of the first Mrs. Graham, but the second Mrs. Graham has made me feel really good again. If there's ever anything I can do for you, please let me know. I will think about you girls every day, for the rest of my life."

Julie sighed and put down her chopsticks. "Jule?" her mother asked. "Are you okay?"

Julie almost jumped in her chair. She had been daydreaming; she had forgotten that she was still sitting at the table with her mother and brother. She looked up. Dennis had soy sauce on his chin; her mother had already begun to stack the dishes. "Oh, sorry," said Julie. "I was just thinking about something."

"You mean you were thinking about some*one,*" said Dennis. "And I know who."

"Kids," said Ms. Hopwood. "Don't start. We've had such a pleasant evening, and the Chinese food was delicious. Let's try to end the day on a positive note, okay?" Ms. Hopwood put down the pile of plates. "Oh, I almost forgot," she said. "Dessert!" She reached into the brown paper bag from Chung's and pulled out a little plastic bag that held three fortune cookies. "One for each of you," said Ms. Hopwood. "And read your fortunes carefully. In my experience, they tend to come true."

"You go first, Mom," said Julie.

"All right," said Ms. Hopwood. She opened the crisp fortune cookie with a loud *crack* and pulled out the slip of paper inside. Then she squinted at it for a moment, because her eyes weren't so good without her glasses. Ms. Hopwood almost never wore her glasses, because they were usually missing—she had a habit of accidentally dropping them behind the cushions of the couch, or leaving them on the counter at the butcher's shop. "Here goes," said Ms. Hopwood. She read the slip of paper aloud. " 'You have a very good imagination.' "

"Wow, that's true!" said Dennis in an excited voice. "You do have a good imagination, Mom! It's like the cookie knows you're a writer!"

Next came Dennis's fortune cookie. He read it out loud. " 'You are an extreme smart person.' " Then he smiled a big smile. "Hey, that one's true too," he said.

"I think whoever wrote this fortune meant to say *extremely*, not extreme," said Ms. Hopwood, "but his or her English wasn't very good."

"But still," said Dennis, "it's like they know me. I skipped a grade, Mom. Everyone says I have a very high IQ. I *am* an extreme smart person."

"All right, Dennis, all right," said Ms. Hopwood. "You don't have to brag. We all know you've got one or two brains in your head." She turned to Julie. "Last but not least," she said, motioning to the remaining fortune cookie. "Let's see if the fortune cookie maker got all three of our fortunes right."

Julie snapped the cookie in half and pulled the fortune out. She read it aloud to her mother and brother. " 'You will find a wife soon,' " Julie read.

Dennis and Ms. Hopwood started laughing. "That's the dumbest thing I ever heard," said Dennis. "Boy, when I read Mom's and my fortunes, I thought maybe these things were for real, but now I've changed my mind. Julie isn't a man. She's not looking for a wife."

"These fortune cookies *are* pretty silly," said Ms. Hopwood. "But still, they taste good." She popped a piece of her cookie into her mouth, and Dennis did the same.

But Julie couldn't stop staring down at the little strip of paper in her hand. Although she couldn't explain this to her mother or brother, she had a funny feeling that maybe the fortune cookie was right: maybe she *would* find a wife soon: a wife for Mr. Graham.

# Chapter Eight

*Dear Box #3468,*

*I read your ad and would like to tell you a little about myself. I am a divorced woman and the mother of four children, all boys. I know that sounds like a lot, but they are very sweet boys, especially the youngest, who is still in diapers. As you can imagine, it's pretty hard to raise four boys all on my own. I work as a nurse at the hospital, but as soon as I get home I begin my second occupation: mother. It would be very nice to meet you. If you'd like to get together, please write back. I don't think it will be possible for us to actually go out on a date—I can't see how I could work that out—but if you'd like to come to the house and visit with me and the boys perhaps during dinnertime, that would be nice. We eat promptly at five* P.M.

*Sincerely,*

*Andrea Shuck*

Susan had just read the letter out loud, and when she finished, everyone was silent. It was Saturday afternoon, and the five friends were back at the Down Street Mall to claim their letters at the *Crier*. There were actually a whole bunch of responses; this was the first one they had opened. They sat at their usual table at Frank's Footlong, with the pile of letters in front of them. Julie had never received that many letters in her life.

"Well," said Alison, "I don't think it's a very good start."

"No, it's not," agreed Trina. "Mr. Graham shouldn't have to stay in that woman's house and have dinner with them at 5:00. He works all day, and then he goes home to his own house. If he's going on a date, it should be a real date."

"Yeah," said Julie.

"He should wear a tie," said Trina.

"He always wears a tie," said Susan. "The point is, this woman doesn't sound like a lot of fun. And Mr. Graham is fun."

"Also," said Stacy, "I don't think he needs four more kids, do you?"

"I saw a movie like that once," said Julie. "It was all about a man and woman who get married, and between them they have ten kids. At first, everyone argues all the time, and hates having to share bedrooms with their stepsisters and -brothers, but after a while, everyone gets along just fine." But she knew that that was just a movie. Mr. Graham was having a hard enough time just managing Anna and Toby; Stacy was right, he didn't need four more kids.

Susan put the letter aside. "Next!" she said, picking up another envelope. She opened it carefully, and held it up to her nose for a moment. "Hmm," she said. "Smells like perfume. A little too *much* perfume. It's like one of those fashion magazines that have ads in them that smell." Susan shrugged. "Well, let's give her a chance," she said. " 'Dear Box #3468,' " Susan began.

> *I was interested to read your personal ad in the* Crier. *I too am a lonely soul looking for someone to love. But in order for me to love him, he has to have certain things.*
>
> 1. *He must be at least 6'1". I hate short men.*
> 2. *He must have hair on his head. His own*

*hair. I cannot stand bald men, or men with toupées.*

3. *He must make a good amount of money. I like to live well. Iowa is a fine place as long as we can also travel to other places, such as Florida, Hawaii, and Europe. By the way, I speak several languages.*

*If the above three things sound like a description of you, then please feel free to write back, and we can arrange to meet. If not, then have a nice life.*

*Yours (maybe),*

*Cecile Deveaux*

*"Have a nice life?"* said Trina when Susan finished reading. "Who does she think she is? And he has to make a lot of money, and he has to be really tall, or else. Boy, what an awful letter."

"I agree," said Julie. "She sounds like a real snob." Julie had no idea of how much money Mr. Graham made, but he certainly *was* tall, and he did have a full head of hair. But if he married Cecile and then started going bald two years after they got married, would she suddenly divorce him? She didn't sound like a very nice person, they all agreed, and they put her letter on top of the first one.

They read through the rest of the letters throughout lunch and during dessert. Stacy went over to the Swedish ice cream place with the name no one could pronounce and brought everyone back cups of vanilla and chocolate swirl. The letters were all beginning to sound alike; some were okay, and there was nothing terrible in them, but no one seemed good enough for Mr. Graham.

Then Julie found one that was different from the others. It was in a small, pale blue envelope, and the handwriting looked very neat and nice. It reminded her of someone's handwriting, but she didn't know whose. Probably it just looked like the kind of handwriting that neat adults had. Julie's mother had terrible handwriting—once, when Julie was in third grade, Ms. Hopwood had written her an absence note, and the teacher thought Julie had faked the note, and had called Julie's home to report it.

Julie sat at the table at Frank's Footlong, and read the letter to herself. All around her, her friends joked and talked, but Julie didn't listen. She was too wrapped up in the letter.

*Dear Box #3468,*

*I have never answered a personal ad before. I never thought I would have to. But my husband died several years ago, and I have been alone since then. In the beginning I didn't want anyone else around, but lately I feel that maybe I am ready to think about dating again. You mentioned children in your ad. If you have children, that's fine, because I do love children and enjoy being around them, even though I don't have any of my own. You also mentioned corny jokes. Well, I may not be the funniest person in the world, but I do enjoy hearing a good joke or watching a funny movie. I think it's important sometimes to laugh and just be silly. Especially when you've had a hard time. And as far as music goes, I love music and used to sing in a chorus. I also listen to CDs a lot at home.*

*You said that you are a widower. I would never want to try to replace your wife, but if you and I liked each other, maybe we could look toward the future. Or at the very least, you could tell me a couple of corny jokes.*

*Sincerely,*

*C. Danner*

Julie put down the letter and thought about it for a moment. Her friends realized that she was staring off into space, and Alison said, "Hey, Jule, you look like you're daydreaming. What's going on?"

"This," said Julie, and she picked up the letter. Then she began to read it aloud, and everyone listened. When she was finished, no one said anything right away. Then Susan let out a long, low whistle, and Stacy said, "Wow."

"She sounds great," Alison finally said.

"I know," said Julie. "She really does. So what do we do now?"

They decided to write back to Miss C. Danner, even though she had included her telephone number. They couldn't possibly fake a telephone call to her, but a letter would do the trick. They sat at their table in the mall and wrote a simple letter that was supposedly from Mr. Graham. It went like this:

*Dear Miss C. Danner,*

*Thank you for your letter. It was my favorite out of all of them. I would like to meet you soon. I don't know where or when yet, but I will write back as soon as I know.*

*Sincerely,*
*Box #3468*

They decided not to sign Mr. Graham's name, because that would be forgery, and they all knew it was against the law. But this way, they weren't doing anything really wrong, were they? That was what they told themselves. The only trouble was, how were they going to get Mr. Graham to show up for a date?

In Mrs. Leff's class, the kids were learning about stars. Their teacher pulled down a map of the night sky, and showed them some of the different constellations. "If you connect the dots, you can see that Cygnus looks like a swan," said Mrs. Leff, "and Ursa Major and Ursa Minor look like a big and a little bear." Julie liked learning about the stars, even though she had trouble memorizing their names. Dennis knew twice as much about the stars as she did, and he hadn't even studied them in school yet. He knew about them just from reading books about astronomy on his own.

"Who would like to tell me about the Milky Way?" Mrs. Leff asked. Nobody's hand shot up. If this was Mr. Graham's class, a dozen hands would be waving in the air, and a dozen people would be calling out, "Me! Me! Pick me!" Mrs. Leff looked slowly around the room. "No one?" she said. "There's no one here who wants to tell me about the Milky Way?"

In the back of the room, a hand went up a few inches. It belonged to Danny Behnke. He never raised his hand for anything. Everyone turned to him with interest.

"Yes, Daniel, go ahead," said Mrs. Leff.

"The Milky Way is, ah . . . a candy bar with chocolate on the outside and nougat and creamy caramel on the inside," he said.

All around the class, kids started to laugh. Julie laughed too. Only Mrs. Leff didn't think it was funny. "You know, class," she said, "when I was in Kansas City, my students turned the classroom into a planetarium, with stick-on stars on the ceiling, and a light show and, oh . . . everything. Other classes came to visit. It was wonderful."

Suddenly, something fell into Julie's lap. It looked like an ordinary note. She peered down at it and unfolded it quietly. It said:

*We the undersigned think that if Mrs. Leff misses Kansas so much, she should go back there. We never want to hear about Kansas again!*

*Signed, Susan Moseby*

Julie looked over at Susan and smiled. Then she took her pen and signed her own name beneath Susan's. After Julie wrote her name, she started to put the note away, to fold it up and slip it inside her notebook, but just then she felt a shadow slowly move across her desk. She knew even before she looked up what had happened. Mrs. Leff was standing over Julie's desk.

"May I see that note?" Mrs. Leff asked. Julie

paused, and then she had to hand it over. When Mrs. Leff finished reading the note, she put it in her pocket. "Julia," she said. "I'd like to see you and Susan after school today." Then she turned and went back up to the front of the room. Everyone was watching. Neither Julie nor Susan had ever gotten into trouble before; this was something new. Everyone stared at them with a look that meant, "Too bad. Too bad. You're in big trouble now." But because nobody else had seen what was written in the note, nobody knew exactly how bad the trouble really was. Julie had an idea that it was very, very bad.

The day passed by slowly. Julie sat and listened to the rest of the lesson about stars, and then Mrs. Leff passed out phonics worksheets. When 11:48 came—the time she and Alison had chosen to meet—Julie didn't dare raise her hand and ask to be excused to go to the water fountain. She knew Ali would be waiting, but she didn't have the nerve to do anything that would make her stand out for the rest of the day. When the lunch bell rang, she was relieved.

On the way to the cafeteria, people kept coming up to Julie and Susan and asking them what had happened. "What was in the note?" asked Adam Lewin. Julie told him what it said.

"Boy," said Adam. "You're in big trouble now."

Julie felt sick. She didn't think she'd be able to

eat at all. She sat at the lunch table and took out her lunch, but it was one of her mother's worst meals: cream cheese and olives on whole wheat. Boring. She closed the bag. Moments later, Alison arrived and slid into the seat beside Julie.

"Where were you?" Alison asked. "I drank so much water from the fountain. I drank and drank, but you didn't show up."

"I got in trouble," Julie said. "I couldn't leave." She and Susan told Alison what had happened, and Alison thought it was pretty bad too.

"I can't believe you wrote that, Susan!" said Alison. "I wonder what she thought. I mean . . . no offense, but it's so . . . *mean*."

"Well, I didn't know Mrs. Leff was going to read it!" said Susan, and her eyes filled up with tears.

"I wonder what she's going to do to you," said Trina, swallowing a bite of her mother's delicious curried chicken salad sandwich.

"Who knows?" said Stacy. "I can't even imagine."

"I've never gotten into trouble before," said Julie. That wasn't entirely true; she had once been caught passing a note in Mr. Graham's class, but that wasn't exactly "trouble." Staying after in Mr. Graham's class meant you had to help clean up, change the shavings in the hamster's cage, and water the plants, all the while being near Mr. Graham. To Julie, that had been fun.

Now she thought about staying after in Mr. Graham's class as though remembering a happy time—a birthday, or Christmas morning. She had a feeling that when Mrs. Leff punished you, it wasn't what you'd call fun.

When lunch ended, Julie and Susan walked together back to the classroom. During reading period, Julie could barely concentrate on her work. She just kept worrying about the end of the day. She kept looking up at the clock, until finally the hands of the clock clicked over into 3:15, setting off the loud, buzzing bell that meant school was over. Kids grabbed their knapsacks and went to get their coats—everyone except the two girls in trouble. Julie and Susan stayed in their seats, looking at each other with worried faces as the classroom slowly emptied. In fifteen minutes the room was completely quiet. Even the school was almost completely quiet; in the distance, Julie could hear the janitor rumbling a trash can down the hall, but that was all. Everyone had gone home.

Up in front of the room, at her desk, sat Mrs. Leff. She was straightening out papers and writing something in her lesson planner, and now she looked up at the girls. "Julia," she said. "Susan. I'd like to talk to you about this." She removed the note from her pocket and unfolded it. Then she read it out loud. It sounded even worse that way. "I know you haven't been very happy being in my class," she said. "Well, I'm sorry about that. But passing notes will not be tolerated. Even if this note had said, 'I wish Mrs. Leff could be our teacher forever and ever,' it wouldn't have made a difference. Note-passing is not allowed."

"Did your students in Kansas ever pass notes, or were they too perfect?" Susan blurted out.

Both Mrs. Leff and Julie looked at her with surprise. "Susan," said Mrs. Leff. "I thought you didn't want to hear about my students in Kansas ever again."

"I'm sorry," said Susan. "I didn't mean it."

"Well," said Mrs. Leff, "I'm afraid I can't let this pass. I'd like you both to stay after school for the rest of the week. You can sit at your desks and read or do your homework. As long as you're quiet, you can work on whatever you choose."

Julie couldn't believe it. It was going to be a whole week of staying after school with Mrs. Leff, and just when Julie and Susan had so much planning to do for Mr. Graham's date. This punishment couldn't have come at a worse time.

"That's all, girls," said Mrs. Leff. "You may go."

Julie and Susan stood up and started to leave. But when they reached the door, Julie heard her say, "Oh, but one more thing." Julie and Susan turned around. "When you stay after school this week," said Mrs. Leff with a tight smile on her face, "no more passing notes, okay?"

# Chapter Nine

*Dear Journal,*

*Well, here I am sitting in Mrs. Leff's classroom with Susan, while the rest of the world (or at least the rest of the school) is out playing video games and eating after-school snacks and watching TV. Mrs. Leff isn't even looking at us; she's grading papers, her head bent down so I can see the part in her hair. Her hair always looks extremely clean.*

*Journal, all I want to be doing is sitting with my friends and figuring out a way to set Mr. Graham up on a date with C. Danner, but instead I'm stuck here. I've already looked at everything on the walls, and let me tell you, it isn't very interesting. There's a chart about the metric system, and a map of the world, and a picture of the human body, the way it would look if it were made of plastic so you could see all the blue veins and the red blood running around inside. Actually, it makes me feel a little dizzy if I look at it for too long.*

*So maybe I should use this time well, and try to come up with a plan for Mr. Graham's date, even without my friends around. These are the possibilities:*

1. *We could just send Miss C. Danner over to Mr. Graham's house. He would have no idea of who she was, and he'd look really confused when he opened the door. But maybe she'd be pretty enough and nice enough that he'd let her in. They'd start talking and they would figure out that somebody had set them up. but by that point they'd already really like each other. We wouldn't have to confess to placing the ad for a really long time—and by then, nobody would be angry with us. In fact, we'd be heroes (or heroines). We'd be the ones who made Mr. Graham fall in love again. We'd be the ones who found a mother for Anna and Toby.*
2. *We could tell Mr. Graham we had a big surprise for him, and that he'd have to*

*wait in a certain place—say, the school parking lot after school—to find out what it was. Then Miss Danner would pull up in her car, and they would meet. Of course, he would know that we had set the whole thing up, but of course he wouldn't be too angry, because he'd fall in love with Miss Danner the minute he saw her.*

3. *We could cancel the whole thing right away. It would never work out, and we'd only get in big trouble. Besides, what if Miss Danner was really fat or something? I don't want you to think I have something against people being overweight—my neighbor Sharon is pretty big, and I like her a lot and barely think of her as fat. (My mother has a fat neighbor character in the "Hathaway" books, but her name is* Karen, *which rhymes with Sharon.) It's just that I care about Mr. Graham, and I want to make him happy. His wife was very pretty, and if he got married again, I'd think he'd want somebody who was pretty too.*

*Well, Journal, that's my list. I'm all out of ideas. I don't think any of my friends really knows how to set up this date, because none of us has been on a date ourselves. That's all I have to write right now. I guess I'll go back to staring at the top of Mrs. Leff's head.*

Julie closed the purple book and looked at the clock. It was almost time to go. She and Susan looked at each other, and then Susan gave a little cough. Slowly Mrs. Leff raised her head, as if coming to the surface after a deep sleep. She squinted at the clock on the wall. "Well, girls," she said, "I guess you can leave. I'll see you tomorrow."

They picked up their knapsacks and walked out into the hall. Julie liked the way the school looked and felt when it was empty. It seemed like a strange and interesting place. She and Susan started walking past Mr. Graham's classroom. They stopped for a moment and peered into the empty room. Even just looking into the room made Julie feel a little sad and sentimental about Mr. Graham. She saw the desk where she had sat last year—it might not have been the *same* desk, but it was in the same spot where hers had been—and she remembered sitting and looking up at the front of the room, and seeing Mr. Graham there. Without really thinking now, she opened the door.

Julie and Susan walked into the room. It

smelled the way she remembered it: of paste and paint and ditto sheets. Suddenly, a voice said, "Well, girls, welcome back."

Julie jumped. There was Mr. Graham; he had been doing something in the coat room, and now he stood facing them with a big smile on his face. "Mr. Graham," said Susan, amazed. "We didn't see you. We were just . . . visiting."

"So, does it look the same?" he asked.

"Kind of," said Julie. "But it also looks different." Even though she hadn't said it very well, she somehow thought that he knew what she meant.

"I'm glad you girls stopped by," said Mr. Graham. "I've been meaning to ask you: are you and your friends interested in doing a little babysitting?"

*"Yes!"* said Julie and Susan at exactly the same second. They looked at each other and laughed.

"Well, that sounds enthusiastic," said Mr. Graham. "I was thinking about this weekend. They're showing one of those full-length cartoons at the movie theater at the mall. I've got some work I need to do. You could go with the kids to the movies, and then take them out for a bite at the mall when it was over, and then I could pick them up. There's a 3:00 show, and it's over at 4:30. I could pick them up at 5:00. How does that sound?"

"Fine," said Julie.

She looked at Susan. Susan seemed lost in thought; suddenly, a slow smile broke out on her face. "Actually," said Susan, "it sounds perfect."

A little later, when they were in the backseat of Susan's mother's car, Susan explained what she had meant. "Don't you *get* it?" she whispered to Julie, but Julie only shook her head. "This is our chance, Jule," she said. "To do you-know-what!"

At first, Julie didn't know what you-know-what was. Then she realized what Susan meant. This was their chance to set Mr. Graham up on a date with Miss Danner! It could all take place at the mall. They could meet each other when he came to pick up Anna and Toby. They wouldn't have a lot of time together, but they could at least meet. Anna and Toby could be off getting ice cream, so Mr. Graham and Miss Danner could have a few moments alone. Of course, the hard part would be getting them to find each other, since Miss Danner didn't know Mr. Graham's name, and Mr. Graham didn't even know he was meeting Miss Danner.

"What are you girls going on about back there?" asked Mrs. Moseby.

"Nothing," said Susan.

"The only thing is," said Julie, "Mr. Graham

wants us to take the kids to the movies *this* Saturday! So that means we only have *three days* to get everything together."

"Wow, you're right," said Susan. "We'd better get moving."

That night, all the friends called each other on the telephone and figured out what to do. Susan typed up a short note to Miss Danner—signed Box #3468, explaining that he would meet her at Frank's Footlong at five o'clock on Saturday afternoon. "What if the letter doesn't get there in time?" Julie asked Susan. "It's just got to," said Susan. "It's just got to."

The girls stayed on the telephone, tying up the lines and making their parents mad. Finally, all the business had been taken care of. The letter would go out first thing in the morning. That night, Julie could barely sleep. She heard her mother writing her novel in the study down the hall—she used a computer and the keyboard didn't make too much noise, but still the gentle clicking was enough to keep Julie up. She also heard her brother Dennis muttering to himself in the next room; probably he was going over some extremely difficult math or science problem. Julie was the only quiet one in the house. She lay in her bed and thought about Mr. Graham. He deserved to be in love, she thought. He deserved to be married.

She wondered what kind of a person she would get married to, when she was grown up. She hoped he was sweet and handsome like Mr. Graham. She wondered if her mother would ever get married again. Her friends certainly thought so; they thought she would marry the make-believe Mr. Katz. But her mother didn't seem in any hurry to get married again, and neither, in fact, did her father. Julie didn't understand how you knew you were ready to get married. She was the only one of her friends whose parents were divorced. She liked going to Ali's house or Trina's house, because everybody was there in one room, sitting down to dinner together—the mother *and* the father.

In a strange way, she felt that she and Mr. Graham had something in common: there was someone missing in both of their families. There was an empty chair at the kitchen table. She could barely remember when her father lived with them, but still it made her sad to think about it. He used to carry her piggyback into bed; that she remembered.

So maybe she and her friends could help make Mr. Graham's house a little less empty. Maybe he would fall in love with Miss Danner and get married and everything would be perfect. Adults fell in love all the time. It was a strange thing that Julie didn't understand, but she knew that it happened. Maybe, she thought as she finally started to get sleepy, it would happen on Saturday.

Julie was very nervous for the rest of the week, and so were Alison, Stacy, Trina, and Susan. Julie met Alison at the water fountain at 11:52 the next day, to talk about it. "What if it doesn't work?" Julie asked. "What if they hate each other?"

"So they hate each other," said Susan. "At least he'll know we tried."

"What if he gets very angry?" Julie asked. "What if he tells us we shouldn't have gotten messed up in his life?"

"Well, we'll tell him that we only wanted to make him happy," said Susan.

"But what if Miss Danner is *awful?*" asked Julie. "What if she's like an old witch?"

"Let's just wait and see, Julie," said Susan. "Let's just wait and see."

But the week went by even more slowly than usual. On Friday afternoon, Julie sat after school in Mrs. Leff's classroom, writing in her journal and watching the clock. Eventually it was time to go. Mrs. Leff slowly straightened out the papers on her desk and then stood up, her chair squeaking a little. "Well, girls," she said. "I guess that's all. Your detention is over for good. I'll see you both on Monday. Have a good weekend."

As Julie and Susan waited outside by the curb for Ms. Hopwood to pick them up, Julie said to Susan, "I wonder what Mrs. Leff does on the weekend."

"She probably tells Mr. Leff how much better her students in Kansas are than him," said Susan, and they both giggled.

"Speaking of husbands," said Susan, "how's Mr. Katz?"

"Who?" Julie asked.

"Mr. Katz," said Susan. "The man you mother's going to marry."

"Oh, Mr. *Katz*. He's . . . fine."

"Do you think they'll get married soon?" asked Susan.

"I don't know," said Julie nervously. "I haven't asked lately."

"Too bad your mother wasn't available to go on a date with Mr. Graham," said Susan. "That would have been great."

"Yeah," lied Julie. "But maybe Miss Danner will be wonderful."

"I can't wait to find out," said Susan.

Saturday morning, Julie woke up to the sound of rain. She groggily sat up in bed and looked out the window. The street was flooding, and water was rushing into the sewers. What a day for a date, she thought. She scribbled some thoughts in her journal, and then she got dressed and went downstairs. Her mother was sitting at the table reading the paper and drinking coffee. As usual on Saturdays, her brother Dennis was still in bed, resting his brain cells.

"Hi hon," said Ms. Hopwood. "Come join me." Julie sat down across from her mother. "There's cereal in the cabinet," her mother said.

"I'm not hungry," said Julie. She wished she could tell her mother what was going on; she felt as though she and her friends had gotten in over their heads, but she had sworn that she wouldn't talk about it, so now she said nothing.

"You okay?" asked Ms. Hopwood.

"Yeah," said Julie.

"It'll be nice for you to see Anna and Toby today," said Ms. Hopwood. "You must be looking forward to that."

Julie realized she'd barely thought about them; she liked Mr. Graham's kids a lot, but she'd been all wrapped up in planning this date. Now she thought about how much fun it would be, taking them to the movies today and then out for hot dogs. But when that was over . . . well, Julie didn't know what was going to happen.

Ms. Hopwood was in charge of the carpool today. At 2:30, she and Julie picked up Stacy, Trina, Alison, and Susan. "I'll see you in the parking lot at 5:15," said Ms. Hopwood as she let them off in front of the mall. She looked Julie straight in the eye. "Have a good day," she said. "I hope everything goes well."

The girls hurried out of the car. Julie closed the car door and her mother drove off into the rain. In a way, Julie wished she was going with her. The five friends stood just inside the mall entrance and looked at each other. "Well," said Susan, "this is it."

They had arranged to meet Mr. Graham and his kids by the giant bird cage in the center of the mall. The cage went all the way up the ceiling. There were finches and parakeets and parrots—lots of brightly colored birds that chattered and squawked all day long. Anna and Toby were peering up to see the birds. Toby was pointing and shouting, naming the different colors he saw. They both looked taller to Julie, even though she'd seen them recently. Mr. Graham wasn't dressed in a suit and tie as usual; instead, he was wearing a blue T-shirt and jeans and a windbreaker. Julie wanted to tell him to get more dressed up, to go home and change before he returned at five o'clock to pick up his kids. "Don't you know this is an important afternoon?" she wanted to say to him. But of course there was no way he could have known.

"Well, girls, I really appreciate this," said Mr.

Graham. "And Anna and Toby are looking forward to it, too. Anna's been talking about all of you all morning."

"Not *all* morning, Daddy," said Anna. "I played with my Barbies, too."

"Oh, that's true, you did play with your Barbies," said Mr. Graham, smiling at the girls. They smiled back.

"Daddy, daddy," said Toby, "I see a *greeeen* bird!" He stretched out the word "green" so far that everybody laughed. Julie felt a little more relaxed. It felt good to be back with the Grahams.

"Well, if everything's in order, I think I'll take off," said Mr. Graham. He crouched down and gave Anna and Toby a hug. "Have a good time today," he said. "I want to hear all about the movie. I'll be back to pick you up at five."

"Remember," said Trina nervously, "we'll be at Frank's Footlong."

"I won't forget," he said. "Well, girls, thanks a lot. Have fun."

And then Mr. Graham turned around and walked away. Everyone watched him go. Toby's lip jutted out as though he were about to cry, so Susan quickly took charge. "Come on," she said, taking Toby and Anna's hands, "it's time for the movie. Who wants popcorn?"

The movie was a full-length cartoon about three kittens who fly in a hot-air balloon to a magical kingdom of dogs. It was meant for little kids, but Julie enjoyed it anyhow. She liked looking over and seeing how involved in the movie Anna and Toby were. When it looked like the kittens might get captured by a pack of German Shepherds, Anna looked as though she might faint with fear, but seconds later, when the kittens managed to escape, as Julie knew they would, Anna was smiling again.

When the movie ended, they left the theater and walked through the mall. In the distance they could hear the birds chattering in their giant cage, and they could smell pizza and caramel apples, and even a faint scent of perfume when they walked past the department store. Then they were in front of Frank's Footlong. It was still early.

Stacy and Trina went up to the counter to buy the food, and everyone else sat at one of the round tables in the back. "That was the best movie I ever saw!" said Anna.

"Me too," said Toby.

"You've hardly seen any movies, Toby," said Anna.

"Oh," said Toby.

The food was put on the table, and everyone ate. Julie cut Toby's hot dog into little triangles so he wouldn't choke. They all sat at the table, but the girls kept nervously looking around.

There was a big digital clock on the wall, and it showed 4:40. Twenty minutes. When Toby and Anna were done eating, Stacy took them across to the other side of the mall, to distract them with ice cream for a while.

Now the clock showed 4:55. Suddenly Julie looked up and saw something. Her eyes widened. "Look who's coming!" she hissed to her friends. It was the last person in the world she wanted to see. Heading right toward Frank's Footlong was, of all people . . . *Mrs. Leff.*

"What's *she* doing here?" said Susan.

"Teachers are allowed to go to the mall," said Alison.

"I know, but of all days," said Susan. "And look, here comes Mr. Graham."

From the opposite direction came Mr. Graham. And sure enough, he and Mrs. Leff noticed each other. He waved a cheerful hello to her. "Oh no," said Trina. "What's going to happen when Miss Danner shows up?" Mr. Graham would be so busy talking to Mrs. Leff that the girls would find it awkward to introduce him to his blind date, thought Julie. This could be a disaster.

Mr. Graham and Mrs. Leff stood together outside Frank's Footlong. "Somebody has to keep an eye out for someone who might be Miss Danner," said Alison.

"I'll go," said Julie. She stood up and went to

the front of the restaurant. It was completely open, like all the storefronts in the mall. She could hear everything that Mr. Graham and Mrs. Leff were saying, just a few feet away.

"Yeah," Mr. Graham was saying. "I'm meeting my kids here. They went to the movies with a few girls who were in my class last year. They're really great girls."

"That's nice," said Mrs. Leff. "I'm meeting . . . well, this is embarrassing. I don't know *who* I'm meeting."

"What do you mean?" asked Mr. Graham.

"Well," said Mrs. Leff, "you'll probably think this is very silly, but I . . . well, I answered a personal ad in the newspaper. I'm supposed to be having a blind date right now. I don't even know his name."

Julie slumped against the wall. How could it *be?* How could it possibly be? She silently slipped away and walked back to the table to join her friends. She had to find a way to break it to them that the wonderful Miss Danner and the awful Mrs. Leff were the *same person*.

# Chapter Ten

Mr. Graham and Mrs. Leff walked into Frank's Footlong together. Mr. Graham looked around for his kids; Mrs. Leff looked around for her date. At the back of the room, Julie, Susan, Trina, and Alison sat at their table with their hearts racing. Julie had just told them what she had overheard, and now everybody was extremely nervous and no one knew what to do. Julie realized that the handwriting in Miss Danner's letter had looked so familiar because she saw it all the time, whenever Mrs. Leff handed back Julie's homework with spelling corrections and comments. But why had Mrs. Leff called herself Miss Danner? What was going on here, anyway?

That was exactly what Mr. Graham wanted to know, too. He caught sight of the girls and left Mrs. Leff to come over to their table. "Hi," he said. "Where are Toby and Anna?" Julie could see a little tension in his smile; since his wife died, he always got nervous when his kids were out of his sight.

"Stacy's getting them ice-cream cones," said Susan. "We were just . . . waiting."

Across the room, Mrs. Leff was sitting and looking at her watch and nervously smoothing down her skirt. Finally Susan stood up. "Mr. Graham," said Susan, "we have something to tell you. Maybe you better call Mrs. Leff over too."

Mr. Graham looked worried. "Is it about Toby and Anna?" he asked.

"No, no, of course not," said Susan. "It's about . . . well, it's about you, and it's about Mrs. Leff's blind date."

"How did *you* know about her blind date?" he asked.

"It's a long story," said Susan. Mr. Graham brought Mrs. Leff over. She looked surprised to see them, and puzzled too, but she sat down beside Mr. Graham and listened.

Everybody talked, cutting in and interrupting each other, or adding things that had been left out. Within ten minutes, the whole story had been told. At first, neither Mr. Graham nor Mrs. Leff said anything. Mrs. Leff looked even more uncomfortable than she did in class.

Mr. Graham spoke first. "Well," he finally said, "that's some story. I hardly know what to say."

"Yes," said Mrs. Leff. "It's quite a story." Suddenly she stood up, and her cheeks were red. "I think I've heard more than enough for one day," she said.

"Catherine, the girls were only trying to help," said Mr. Graham. "They were all in my class last year, and ever since my wife, Sheila, died, they've stuck by me and tried to make things a little easier. This . . . blind date—they didn't mean any harm by it. Although, of course, things did get pretty messy."

"I'll say," said Mrs. Leff.

"I know it must be hard," said Mr. Graham softly, "to be on your own in a new place."

"Yes," said Mrs. Leff. "It is hard. Very hard." Then she looked at everybody and sighed deeply. "Well," she said, "I guess you girls want to know why I put a different name on my letter." It *had* occurred to Julie, although she didn't dare ask. "Danner is my maiden name," said Mrs. Leff, "and the C. stands for Catherine. I use my maiden name often, but I've decided to keep my husband's name at my job. At the school in Kansas, I was known as Mrs. Leff, and it's what I feel most comfortable being called by my students." She paused. "Susan and Julie," she said, "in that note you passed in class, you said you wondered why I didn't go back to Kansas if I was so happy there. Well, it's true, I did love my school there, and the boys and girls in my class. But you know, I had sad memories too. I had a husband and he died. I decided that it was a good idea to make a new start, to have a new place to live, a new job. So I moved here. I know it hasn't been the best year so far, has it?" She tried to smile. "And I haven't been the best teacher in the world. Certainly," she said, "I haven't been anything like Mr. Graham."

"Well . . ." said Julie.

"Well . . ." said Susan.

But they couldn't go on. "You know," said Mrs. Leff, "even though I talk about how great my students in Kansas were, it doesn't mean they were perfect. Nobody is perfect." Her voice got quiet now. "Especially me," she said. "But I'd like a chance to put all of that behind me. I'd like to be happy here in Iowa City. And you do seem like a nice bunch of students. Maybe I just haven't given you enough of a chance yet."

Just then, Anna and Toby came running up to the table, their faces streaked with chocolate. Stacy followed. When she saw everybody sitting together, Mrs. Leff included, she looked really confused. "I'll explain later," whispered Alison, and Stacy sat down. Anna and Toby climbed into their father's lap.

"Daddy," said Anna. "You should have seen the movie we saw! There were five kittens, and they got lost in a balloon, and they landed in a town where there were all these big, mean dogs!"

"Yeah, we saw dogs, Daddy!" said Toby.

"That's wonderful, kids," said Mr. Graham, and he kissed both of his children on the tops of their heads. Then he turned back to the girls. "As for me," he said, "you know, it was a nice idea you had, to try to find me someone new to marry But I'm nowhere near thinking about that. I've got a pretty full life already with these two kids, chocolate stains and all. They're enough for me right now. If a time comes, somewhere in the future, when I'm ready to think about getting married again, well, I'll know who to call."

Nobody knew what to say. Julie looked at Mr. Graham, watched him sitting with his two kids, saw the red hair that he had passed down to both of them, and she thought: they're a family. Then she thought of her own family, her father in L.A., her mother and her brother, waiting at home. She didn't see her father enough, and Dennis could be very annoying, boy genius that he was, and her mother didn't know how to cook or keep her pocketbook from getting lost, but they were her family. And then she thought of Mrs. Leff, who didn't have a husband or any kids. But she had the students she taught, and maybe, if she started to loosen up a little during the year, they would want to get to know her, the way Mr. Graham's students always wanted to get to know him. It was true, Mrs. Leff would never be quite like Mr. Graham, but then again, no one would.

That night, the girls all had dinner at the Hopwoods'. Julie's mother ordered out again—pizza for everyone—and as they sat at the table, they reluctantly told Ms. Hopwood the story about trying to find Mr. Graham a wife. She was shocked. "Girls," she said, "that's grown-up business. You should have known that."

"But Mr. Graham wasn't really angry," said Julie. "He was glad that we tried to help."

"Well, he's a very patient man," said Ms. Hopwood. "But sometimes you girls go too far. I think you need to let the Grahams figure some of their problems out on their own."

"It's too bad you couldn't have gone out on a date with him, Ms. Hopwood," said Stacy.

"Yeah," said Trina. "It's too bad about Mr. Katz."

"Mr. *who?*" asked Ms. Hopwood, and everyone turned to stare at Julie. She sank several inches into her seat. Apparently, there was a lot more explaining to do.

"Mr. Katz," Julie stammered. "He's this . . . well . . ." She took a deep breath. "He's the guy I said you were going to marry!"

"But I don't know anyone by that name," said Ms. Hopwood.

"I know," said Julie, and now she was in tears. "I made him up. I didn't want you to go out with Mr. Graham, so I said you were engaged."

Her friends kept staring. "Boy," said Alison in a quiet voice, "you lied, Jule. You actually lied to us."

"Julie's a prevaricator," said Dennis. "That's what you are, Julie. A prevaricator."

"A what?" asked everyone. Dennis knew all the hardest words.

"It means a liar," said Ms. Hopwood. "And thank you, Dennis, I think we can all live without your commentary."

"I'm really sorry, guys," Julie said. "I had to make *something* up. I didn't want my mom going out with my favorite teacher in the world. I mean, how would you feel?"

Everybody was quiet. This was so embarrassing, being caught in a big lie in front of her friends and her mother and Dennis. Julie wished she could just run away from the table and go hide in her bedroom upstairs, but she knew she couldn't.

"I guess I wouldn't feel so great about it, if it were my mother," said Trina slowly.

"Me neither," said Stacy.

Her friends were starting to understand. It would be all right, Julie knew. "Come on," said

Susan, "let's talk about something else. We can pick on Julie tomorrow, okay?"

Julie wanted to hug her friends. The only one she still worried about a little was Alison. Julie knew that she would have some serious making up to do the next morning when they met at the water fountain at 11:58.

That night, when Julie was getting ready for bed, she could hear her brother talking to himself in the next room, practicing vocabulary words. "Prevaricator," he said again, and she winced. But then he went on to other words that she'd also never heard of: *proselytize,* and *procrastinate*. He seemed to be up to the *p*'s in his dictionary.

Julie folded tomorrow's clothes over her chair, shut off the overhead light, and got into bed. In a moment her mother came in. "Hey," her mother said softly. "Are you okay?"

"Yeah," said Julie. "We really blew it today. And I blew it too."

"Oh, honey," said her mother. "Did you really expect that Mr. Graham would fall madly in love with a woman he'd never met before?"

"I guess not," said Julie.

"Love doesn't work like that," said Ms. Hopwood. "At least not most of the time. It hasn't for me, since your father and I got divorced, has it?"

"I guess not," said Julie again.

"Love takes a long time," said Ms. Hopwood. "And it happens in ways you never expect. Sometimes people *do* fall in love when they go on a blind date, but most of the time people fall in love because they happen to meet each other and like each other very much. It's like anything else—like becoming friends, for instance. Nobody set you up with Alison—you just became best friends on your own." Her voice got softer. "And nobody told you that you would think Mr. Graham was the greatest teacher in the world. You just felt that way on your own. That's the way things happen—you just have feelings."

"Yeah," said Julie. "I guess you're right."

"And as for me and Mr. Katz," said her mother, "well, I've been thinking. He sounds like a pretty neat guy."

"He is," said Julie. "I mean, that's the way I pictured him. He's got brown hair and he wears nice sweaters. And he's got two cats, named Anthony and Gwendolyn."

Her mother smiled. "You made all this up," she said.

"I told you already, I lied," said Julie.

"Well, yes, I know," said Ms. Hopwood. "But what I'm saying is that you made all this up, just the way I make things up when I write my novels. You made up a character—Mr. Katz—and you know all about him. Honey, I know you think you're the one in the family who doesn't have any real talent, but I have a feeling that you might have a talent for writing."

"I wrote down the story about Mr. Katz," said Julie. "In the journal that you gave me."

"Well, I'd like to read it sometime," said her mother. "If you ever feel like showing it to me."

Julie smiled. "Yeah, I'd like that," she said. "If you don't make fun of my spelling."

Her mother leaned forward and kissed her. "You're a good kid," she whispered. "A lousy matchmaker, but a good kid. And maybe you'll turn out to be a pretty good writer, too." Then she stood up, walked out, and softly closed the door.

Julie lay there for a while, thinking about everything that had happened, the thoughts crowding her head, coming to her all at once. Her mother was right: Mr. Graham would have to fall in love on his own. But maybe Julie could sort of keep an eye on him; maybe Dennis could give Julie daily reports on Mr. Graham. Then maybe she wouldn't be so jealous that her brother was in Mr. Graham's class. Maybe she'd even start to like it. It would be a way of keeping Mr. Graham in her life, just a little bit.

And as far as Mrs. Leff went—or Miss Danner—Julie felt as though she might even start to like her one of these days. It was true that she was unfriendly, but that was only because she was lonely. Of course, if she mentioned her students in Kansas one more time, Julie felt that she'd have to scream. But maybe Mrs. Leff would meet someone else wonderful through the *Crier*. Or maybe Julie and her friends could try to find her a husband. Stacy's cousin Cindy over in Dubuque had parents who were divorced, and Stacy said her uncle was really nice. Maybe the girls could introduce him to Mrs. Leff, and they could go out on a blind date. . . .

Or maybe not, Julie thought. After everything that had happened that day, it was probably a terrible idea. They would have to stop being matchmakers and go back to being sixth-graders. That wasn't so bad, was it? Julie thought. They weren't in Mr. Graham's class anymore, and she knew that would always make her sad, but the phrase "sixth-graders" sounded pretty amazing. Julie and her friends were getting older, and next year they would actually be in junior high.

It was getting late now, and Julie supposed she really ought to go to sleep, but she wasn't quite ready. She switched on the reading lamp beside her bed, and picked up the purple journal from her night table. Julie turned to the next clean page, and then she started to write.